THE STAR WANDERER

She wanders among stars.
Through a billion solar systems seeded across
universal space she moves with majesty and grace.
She is vast, larger than many of the planets she
monitors.
She will never die.
She is immortal.
Now, at this precise moment in space and time, her goal
is to claim a man of Earth.
His name is Logan.

LOGAN'S
SEARCH

William F. Nolan

LOGAN'S SEARCH
A Bantam Book/October 1980

ISBN 0-553-13805-7

Published simultaneously in the United States and Canada

Bantam Books are published by Bantam Books, Inc. Its trademark, consisting of the words "Bantam Books" and the por-
trayal of a bantam, is Registered in U.S. Patent and Trademark
Office and in other countries. Marca Registrada. Bantam
Books, Inc., 666 Fifth Avenue, New York, New York 10103.

PRINTED IN THE UNITED STATES OF AMERICA

0 9 8 7 6 5 4 3 2 1

For my parents,

Michael Cahill Nolan (1877–1965)
Bernadette Kelly Nolan (1894–1979)

who are alive, somewhere, in this universe—

with love and gratitude.

Because of you,   Logan runs.

PREFACE

With the publication of this novel, the Logan trilogy is complete. All three novels are interrelated in theme, concept, and characters, but each is separate and self-sustaining. *Logan's Run* was first published in 1967. Ten years later, in 1977, *Logan's World* was released. And now, finally, *Logan's Search* rounds out the trilogy. Together, the three Logan novels possess an organic unity that is directly linked to our present era. They form a metaphor for what critic Arthur Knight has termed "the computerized, restrictive takeover by corporate wealth that most of us feel is governing our lives." In fighting, with compassion and sensitivity, against this restrictive system (as I have reshaped it in futuristic terms), Logan the Sandman/runner has become a genuine culture hero.

Each culture in history selects its own generational heroes. No amount of publicity or promotional hype can create a popular phenomenon if the audience is not responsive. Heroes can never be *imposed* on a world culture; they emerge from a combination of elements relating to psychological mass appeal, emotional needs, and a specific political climate. Springing from these complex roots, the popular hero invariably reflects the idealism of a particular culture.

I did not set out to create such a hero. In writing the Logan trilogy, I chose certain societal basics—age, death, war, population pressure, youth power, and mechanistic control—and projected them into a repressive future where every citizen's life span is brief and state-decreed. My warning is subliminal, presented within a frame of pure action-adventure. Overt preaching can be deadly, in or out of novels. Philosophically, the

Logan novels present character-within-action, message-within-movement. They were written to be fun, to entertain, but with an under-surface solidity of idea and concept. *Cinefantastique* critic Scott Schumack summed up the world of Logan as "an alloy of style and substance . . . a fusion of adventure story and didactic satire."

The tri-novel saga, therefore, has depth; layered surfaces exist, onionlike, beneath a skin of speed and glitter. But the question is: What, precisely, has elevated the character of Logan 3 to the rarefied status of a culture hero?

Universally, we fear age, sickness, and early death. When these root fears are combined with our basic mistrust of an overpowerful police state, we have a natural arena for rebellion.

In the timeless tradition of all culture heroes, Logan rebels. He refuses to be struck down in his youth, refuses to allow a coldly mechanistic society to defeat and destroy him. With Jessica, his life's love—and a woman strong within herself—he runs. The psychic nerve of self-survival has been touched.

There is a line in *Logan's Search*. Ballard says to Logan, "With you, we run, we survive." That line is the key to my trilogy, to Logan's mass appeal. We outrun death with him. Symbolically, *we* survive. He renews our oft-assaulted faith in the success of personal rebellion against encroaching, dehumanizing authority.

Logan's adventures are life-affirming, love-affirming. They speak out, through a glass darkly, for the joy of living. They defy a life-denying system. The problems faced by Logan reflect the anxieties of our own society during the past two decades.

Logan is a culture hero because he ultimately defeats the murderous system that shaped him; he is a force for positive action in this troubled era of doubt and confusion, when most of our actual flesh-and-blood "heroes" run on feet of clay.

And I'm damned proud of him.

I want to acknowledge the many readers and viewers who have written me about Logan and Jessica, collected Logan material, formed clubs, printed their own fan magazines. . . .

An author writes to communicate his personal visions, to reach the widest possible audience. I have been fortunate in accomplishing this goal. It is gratifying to know that Logan, as a pop-culture hero, has touched the lives and minds of hundreds of thousands around the world who have shared his adventures in these novels, on the big screen, in magazines, and on television.

I thank each and every one of you—deeply and sincerely.

William F. Nolan
Woodland Hills, California

Attempt the end, and never stand to
    doubt;
Nothing's so hard but search will find
    it out.

—Robert Herrick

She is a star wanderer.

She moves with authority and majesty and grace through a billion solar systems seeded across universal space.

She is vast, larger than many of the planets she monitors. Beyond her primary warp-drive hyperspace capabilities, she is equipped with no less than one thousand massive ion-thrust units exceeding the combined power of a dozen suns.

Superbly shielded, her multilayered metal skin is impenetrable. Nothing can harm her.

She will never die.

She is immortal.

And her goal now, at this precise moment in space and time, is to claim a man of Earth.

His name is Logan.

SOMETHING OUT THERE

The unborn child was restless. He kicked out at the pulsing red darkness surrounding him, awakening his mother. Her voice murmured softly to him; her hands pressed inward, soothing him. . . .

"He's getting impatient," said Logan, now awake also. "Wants out." He smiled at Jessica.

She nodded. "He'll just have to wait his turn, like everyone else," she said, massaging her flesh in a rhythmic manner designed to calm the child.

"Well, he's still got a few weeks in there," Logan said, patting her swollen stomach. He suddenly looked serious. "It's not too late to change his name."

She sighed, saying nothing.

Logan got up, moved to the window, glanced out at the sweep of night sky. The moon was full, riding free beyond massed clouds. Its light defined his face in hard, sharp planes.

Jessica rose to stand beside him, pressing the soft swell of her body against him.

"It's what I want," she said softly. "We lost Jaq—and now it's as if . . . we have him back again."

"But that's not really true," said Logan. "You *know* that each child is different." He turned to her, cupping her face gently in the moonlight. "Jaq is gone forever. It took us a long time to accept it, but he's *gone*, Jess."

"I know," she said, lips trembling.

He leaned to kiss her, running his right hand slowly over the miraculous life-swell of flesh. "This is *new* life—a new human being. . . ."

1

Jessica nodded. "I understand what you're saying
... really I do." She hesitated. "It's just that ... calling him Jaq will mean a lot to me."

Logan kissed her cheek very gently. "Fine. No
more objections."

And they stood together in the moon-glimmered
bedroom in the mansion on the hill above the dry Potomac, not speaking as the drifting clouds massed sol-
idly, shutting out the light.

It appeared in the sky over Old Washington the
next morning—small, silvery, glinting—a strange metal
dragonfly dropping swiftly toward Maincamp.

The Wilderness People were alarmed. Their vow
of nonviolence, sworn after the deaths at Crazy Horse
in the Dakotas, severely limited their ability to defend
themselves against outside attack. They had no offensive weapons, no effective way to fight an enemy.

However, as they soon discovered, this was no enemy.

A tall man, bare-headed and weaponless, in torn
grays, climbed weakly from the control pod of a silver
skybug. Its rotor blades whispered to silence behind
him as he advanced on the camp at a stumbling walk.
He was gaunt-fleshed; his spindly legs would barely
support him. Beard stubble darkened his thin cheeks,
and his eyes were desperate.

Logan caught the man as he half fell to one knee,
helping him the rest of the way into camp. A group of
shouting Wilderness children danced around them, excited by the event. Logan spoke sharply, and the children melted back, clearing a space for the exhausted
stranger.

Several primary members of the camp moved out
from the central chambertent to face the newcomer.

He blinked at them. "Who—who leads here?"

"We have no leader," said Fennister.

His woman, Lisa, stood at his shoulder, nodding.
"We are all equal here," she said.

"We function as a group, a single unit," added
Mary-Mary.

The gaunt man smiled weakly. "Idealists!"

"Realists," corrected Logan. "We know what absolute power can do. We've had enough of it." He looked down at the gaunt man, who had propped his back against a tree; the stranger sat in a slumped posture, drained of energy.

"Who are you?" Fennister asked him. "Why have you come here?"

"My name is Karrick 3. I'm from the Chicago Complex."

"You're a long way from home," Logan said.

"I've been searching for help." Karrick's voice broke. "We—we're all starving back there! We must have food!"

"We've barely enough for ourselves," said Fennister.

"There are many children here," said Mary-Mary. "With new ones coming." She glanced significantly at Logan.

"Others have asked for help," said Lisa, "but we were forced to refuse."

"But you *must* help us!" Karrick pleaded. "I could find no one . . . there's nowhere else for me to go." He looked in desperation toward Logan. "You call yourselves realists. All right, then—let's talk trade." He hesitated. "What do you need most?"

"What we always need," said Logan. "Medical equipment . . . healing drugs . . . lab supplies."

"We have all that," said Karrick. "When the food supply failed, the Scavenger packs abandoned Chicago. We have free access to the medshops."

Logan turned to Fennister, eyes intense. "Even if we have to ration food this winter," he said, "it will be worth it for medical security. Five died last year because we lacked proper supplies."

Fennister rubbed his cheek, thinking. Then he raised a hand. The Wilderness People grouped in around them. "An offer," Fennister declared loudly, so that all could hear. "Medical supplies for food. How do you vote?"

A muttering. A brief cross-discussion of terms. A hand count was made: the vote was almost unanimous.

"We trade," said Fennister.

Karrick smiled in exhausted relief. Then he drew a long breath, his lips tight. "I'll leave tonight."

"You're in no condition to handle a ship," Logan said. "I'll make the flight—with signed authority from you."

"Agreed." Karrick sighed, extending a thin-boned hand. As Logan shook it, Karrick had tears in his eyes. "Thank you," he said softly.

"Get some rest," Logan told him, pressing the man's trembling shoulder. "I'd say you've earned it!"

As he lifted away from Old Washington in the silver skycraft, Logan experienced a sharp sense of guilt at having left Jessica. With the new baby coming she had not wanted him to undertake the flight, claiming that she needed him with her, psychologically, at this special time in her life.

"But I'm the only qualified pilot at Maincamp," he'd argued. "It's a short trip. I'll be back home in plenty of time to greet young Jaq!"

"Let Karrick make the flight. In a few days he'll be strong enough."

"I volunteered. I gave my word."

And then she had shivered, looking at him with sudden fear in her eyes. "Don't go, Logan." She crossed both arms over her rounded life-flesh in a protective gesture. "I'm afraid."

"You'll be *fine* here," he'd assured her. "Lisa and Mary-Mary will look after you."

"No—it's *you* I'm afraid for. There's . . . something out there."

The phrase had startled him. "What are you saying?"

"I—don't know exactly." She'd groped for words. "But . . . it's as if I'm tuned in to something. . . ."

And she had shivered again.

"Hey, hey . . ." He had taken her gently into his arms. "There's nothing out there between me and the Chicago Complex but a lot of empty sky. Now, no more of this, hear me? Let's have a smile out of you!"

And she had smiled.

But the fear had remained in her eyes.

* * *

The night was dark with stormclouds, the moon deep-buried. Bad flying weather—with a hard rain beginning to slash at the canopy. The wind was choppy at this altitude, slapping the little skybug in staggered gusts.

Logan checked the tie-down straps on the two heavy crates of food beside him in the cockpit. Fully secure. No problem.

The bug was quick and totally reliable, with twice the cruise range of his own paravane—and with power enough to climb above the storm into clear weather.

The storm . . . Maybe *that's* what Jess was worried about, thought Logan, as he set the controls for maximum ascent. Maybe pregnant women can feel bad weather in their bones.

Odd, though, the way she'd phrased it: ". . . something out there."

If not the storm, what then?

Just what *had* she sensed?

Location?
Directly below, and climbing.
Intersect point?
Immediate.
Stabilize. Prepare to encounter.

Logan was puzzled. According to the controls, he should be seeing moon-clear night sky above him, but apparently there was a malfunction.

The entire arc of sky within view range was obscured with . . .

Not clouds. A shape. Dark . . . all-encompassing . . .

Logan pressed forward, face against the canopy, peering upward.

He was stunned.

He'd never seen anything so gigantic! Its size was absolutely incredible, beyond rational acceptance. In simply contemplating it, Logan was swept by vertigo.

A ship. Some kind of mammoth alien starcraft moving through our solar system.

No, not moving. Stabilized. Dark and utterly motionless. Nonreflective surface. No lights. No sound.

Silent and immense above him.

". . . Something out there."

Then, abruptly, with painful brightness, an energy beam flared from the hull of the great ship, bathing Logan's small skybug in a fire circle of illumination so intense that he twisted in agony, shielding his eyes.

Get away! Now!

Gasping, he threw himself forward, fingers clawing at the descent lever.

No response. The controls were frozen, locked tight.

Above him, a seamless mouth opened in the underbelly of the great starship—and Logan felt his small craft being sucked upward with impossible force.

His breath was snatched from his lungs; he was flung savagely backward against the control seat.

Logan tried to cry out as the darkness engulfed him.

Or was this black horror of a ship eating him alive?

Movement.

Something touching him . . .

Something speaking to him . . . a soundless inner voice: *Open your eyes, Logan 3.*

Logan opened his eyes to a spin of blazing colors. He blinked, and the colors steadied—became illuminated dials, glittering wall switches, blinking relays. . . . Around him, the room seemed alive, vibrating to the tick and hum of alien machinery.

The mental image struck him with sudden impact: *alien.*

Again, the soundless telepathic voice: *To you, that is what we are, Logan. Just as your race is alien to ours.*

Logan had awakened naked, in a sitting position, his body softly supported by a cluster of flaring, free-floating diamonds—or what *seemed* to be diamonds. Now, with a soft clicking, the diamonds shifted—and Logan found himself standing, in semishock, facing a large glowing crystal set into the wall directly ahead of him.

The crystal pulsated with banded patterns of light, radiating energy like a thousand tiny suns.

Some kind of force field, thought Logan.

A door, Logan. Leading to us.

Logan stepped toward it, was jolted back.

His words were hard, angry: "Let me through. . . . Let me see you!"

Stand as you are. Do not move. We will come to you. But, first . . .

From the arched ceiling a transparent cone whispered down to settle over Logan's naked body. He felt trapped inside the cone, like an insect in a bottle.

For your protection. Without it, we could not approach you.

The crystal began misting away in a myriad of brightly dissolving particles.

They were coming.

Logan could feel his heart beating wildly. His mouth was dry. What would he see? What type of monstrous life form would confront him? Would he be repulsed, stunned, sickened?

His thoughts brought a reply: *We are creatures of beauty, Logan. Like your sun.*

And so they were: pure beings of dazzling energy. Logan drew up a hand to shield himself against their combined brilliance, slitting his eyes to see them—three of them—rippling and merging, flowing now together, now apart, in a core of incredible light and heat.

Now you understand the need for your protection. If we removed the cone, our radiance would blind you—and your flesh would melt to instant ash.

Logan realized that the voice he seemed to hear inside his head came from *all* of them; there was no separation of tone. They communicated mentally as a single entity.

"Why am I here?"

You are here because of what you are—a Sandman who defied a life-destroying system, who outran it,

outwitted it, and finally destroyed it. You ended com-
puter rule on Earth.

"Not me; Ballard," Logan said. "It began with
Ballard. I just finished what he started. And I was not
alone—there were many others . . . Jess, Mary-Mary,
Fennister, Jonath of the Wilderness People. . . ."

We know of them. But you were the force that
brought the Thinker to final ruin.

"How? How do you know about all this?"

We have ways of monitoring your world as we
monitor others. Our powers are vast—quite beyond
your imagination.

Logan felt his adult self being stripped away.
Here, facing these fantastic beings, he had regressed to
the level of a child in Nursery. He felt small, totally
powerless; he knew nothing of the countless starworlds
swarming their universe.

He had never concerned himself with suns beyond
Sol, with planets beyond this solar system. . . . They
were right: all this was, literally, beyond his imagination.

But he pulled himself up from the mental gulf
that separated them; he forced himself to accept the reality of the moment, however bizarre. He had many
answers to find.

"What do you want with me?" Logan asked them.

We have chosen you for a mission. If you accom-
plish it successfully, you will be released, sent back to
Earth—to your woman and your son.

"Then . . . you know about Jessica . . . about
Jaq?"

Of course.

"Is she aware of what's happened to me?"

No one knows. You are free to tell them when
you return. There was a slight pause. *If you return.*
The chance for failure is high, since the mission is
quite dangerous.

"What does it involve?"

You will replace another human from Earth.

"For what purpose?"

Your questions will be answered after you have
undergone alteration.

Logan recoiled from the thought: they were going to *change* him, use their technology to alter his body and personality. A form of death.

He must escape!

Escape! The alien voice seemed to mock him. *There is absolutely no escape from us. Surely you realize how totally unrealistic such a concept is in these circumstances?*

Logan nodded wearily. Again, they were right. There was no escape. He would do exactly as they bade him.

He would accept alteration.

A transfer machine will take you to our mothercraft, where you will proceed through the alteration process.

Logan blinked. "Then—this isn't your ship?"

Only one of our smaller drones, equipped to enter your atmosphere.

Small! Logan had been amazed at the gigantic size of the craft. What must the mothership be like?

You will soon see for yourself.

And the sun-bright beings flowed back through the wall.

Their radiance was gone.

The crystal reshaped itself.

The cone lifted away from his body.

And Logan was alone once more in humming darkness.

TO ANOTHER LIFE

The transfer machine that came for Logan resembled a large, highly glossed seashell from the beaches of Earth. The forward section of its opalescent shell-surface folded back—and Logan settled warily into an organic passenger seat that molded itself to the contours of his body.

The shell sealed itself around him and glided into silent motion, moving smoothly through an exit port and along a narrow tongue of metal that linked the drone to the mothership.

Although Logan was completely encased within the machine, he had a clear field of vision through its transparent forward surface—and the effect was awesome.

Indeed, the drone craft was minuscule in comparison to its great mother. The titan's subtly curved interior seemed limitless, rolling above and below Logan for miles—a metallic world of shining alien substance far beyond human engineering.

They moved faster.

As the shell's momentum continued to build, outside details coalesced into a swift blur of silver gray. They were now rushing through this mammoth, hollow world at mind-numbing velocity.

Logan closed his eyes . . . experienced dizziness . . . nausea. . . . In the violent onslaught of speed his body was thrust inexorably back into the coutoured seat; he was assaulted by forces that threatened to burst his bones, sunder his flesh. . . .

Relief came in the form of a cool needle-stab, rendering him instantly unconscious.

When he awoke, the alteration process had been painlessly completed.

Logan sat up on the ship's medtable. He was wearing the black uniform of a Sandman.

Behind their protective wall of shimmering crystals, the three alien light-forms pulsed and merged, sending their words into Logan's newly awakened mind: *You are displeased, Logan?*

Because the crystal wall muted their radiance, Logan was able to look directly at his captors without shielding his eyes. They were like miniature suns, flickering cores of flame, without solid form.

"You didn't tell me I was replacing a Sandman," he said. "The system's dead. This uniform is meaningless now on Earth."

Not where you go.

"The Thinker's dead, and the world is free," declared Logan. "The Sandmen are finished."

Same reply: *Not where you go.*

Logan was confused; he reached up to finger the bones of his chin . . . his cheeks and forehead . . . seeking the new shape of flesh. But it was impossible to tell what they had done to him.

"Who am I? I want to see myself. A mirror—do you have one?"

In the adjoining chamber.

To Logan's right, a tall silver slidepanel whispered back.

Your mirror is there.

Logan entered the chamber, the panel sliding closed behind him. He stood in total darkness, nervous and uncertain.

What would he see? Whose face did he wear? Would it be a Sandman he'd known at DS Headquarters?

A sudden pillar of light. Inside the pillar, suspended between floor and ceiling and supported by clusters of floating diamonds, was the naked figure of a sleeping man.

Logan moved closer to stare in silent shock at the Earthman he was to replace.

Your mirror, Logan 3.

He was staring at himself!

Logan slowly circled the figure. "Is this . . . some kind of *robot?*"

He is quite real. A human of flesh and blood, as you are.

Logan studied the face of the sleeping man: his own. The hands: his own. The body: his own. Hair, mouth, curvature of cheek and chin: his own.

"You've altered another man to look exactly like me!"

The reverse is true, the aliens told him. *We have altered you to look exactly like him. Since he is over a decade younger than you, we had to erase certain lines in your face, subtly rework your body flesh, alter the pores of your fingers to match his. Now the two of you are identical.*

The pillar gradually dimmed as the Logan mirror-figure dissolved in a soft flicker of diamonds. Fading . . . gone . . . swallowed in blackness.

The silver wallpanel once again hushed open behind Logan, and he walked numbly back into the med-chamber.

He faced the aliens.

It was necessary for you to see him in order to understand your mission.

Logan's jaw was hard-set; he glared at the flickering flame shapes. "Damn you! What kind of trick is this?"

No trick, Logan. The man you saw is a younger version of yourself.

"Version?"

From another Earth. A parallel world, in which Sandmen still pursue runners. On that world he was fanatically loyal to the system of computer-directed death at twenty-one—the same system you helped end forever on your own planet.

Logan felt himself caught in a dream from which he could not wake—yet he knew this was no dream. It was real. It was all actually happening to him. To maintain his base of emotional sanity, he had to keep telling himself this, over and over. No dream . . . no dream . . .

From the wall, a shapechair appeared.

Sit down, Logan. Watch what we show you. Watch—and listen.

Without choice, Logan obeyed. The chair shaped itself around him as the room darkened.

Holographic images materialized: an emerald universe of endless depth. Like a mute god, Logan sat surrounded by an infinity of stars and planets, silver-dusted galaxies, exploding nebulae. . . .

The cool, emotionless voice of the aliens entered his mind: *Each planet in universal space is paralleled by many other near-identical worlds. We are concerned in monitoring certain of these alternate worlds, utilizing basic vibrations in the space-time continuum to effect a passage from one world to another on a direct line. This direct line limits our activities and knowledge on any given world.*

"Just what does that mean?"

It means we cannot enter the past or future of any world. We can monitor them only in their current, present-time status.

As the aliens spoke, their words were enhanced for Logan within the holographic universe. A tiny craft, representing the alien starship, hovered above a twin solar system on a direct line between two Earths. The configurations of the planets were identical.

With the elimination of a computerized death system, your Earth has now stabilized. It is this second planet that now concerns us. We know that something—or someone—controls its world-computer programming. A dark force, possibly supernatural, guides the system.

One of the two tiny Earths darkened, as if denied the light of the sun.

This dark force must be rooted out and destroyed. We feel that you are uniquely qualified for this mission. For you, it will be much like a time trip—a return to your yesterdays.

Now the holographic show was over. The images died.

Logan swung back to face the aliens.

We sense confusion. You have many questions. Ask them.

"I'm just one man. How can I change a world?"

You changed your own.

"I don't see the logic of this. With the powers you possess, why not simply brainwash the other me and send *him* back to change his own planet?"

Our powers are limited. We have no way of effectively overcoming young Logan's lifelong conditioning. You must take his place.

"And do exactly what?"

Prior to our removing him, young Logan had been preparing for a ritual known as Godbirth, which for certain Sandmen of high rank is an alternative to Deep Sleep. We think that through Godbirth you will be able to penetrate the planet's central power base.

"Will I be given any special weapons?"

No weapons. But, since there appears to be a form of indoctrination connected with this ritual, we have provided mental shielding. You are now immune to any mind technique they may attempt to employ.

Logan found the concept of a double world hard to assimilate: the same, yet not the same.

"Is there a Ballard on this Earth?"

Ballard does not exist. No Sanctuary Line. No base in Washington. No escape rockets at Cape Steinbeck.

"Then—there's no Sanctuary for runners!"

A few female runners seem to have vanished, but we have not been able to determine their fate. They may still be alive somewhere on the planet. There is much we do not know.

"What of Francis? If Ballard does not exist—"

Each world has its own structure, Logan. Francis is very real on this world, a key Sandman, a Master of the Gun. He has also been selected for Godbirth, and will accompany you through the ritual.

"But as a fanatic to the system, won't he be dangerous?"

Not at first. He is young Logan's best friend. Thus, he will trust you. Eventually, of course, you will have to kill him.

"And just what becomes of young Logan?"

We shall return him safely to his world as we shall return you to yours. But only if your mission is a success. His life, therefore, depends on you.

Logan's emotions toward his duplicate were mixed: he didn't want to be responsible for the death of this young man. He would, in effect, be killing himself. Yet, face to face, one would be forced to destroy the other, runner against Sandman. A paradox, the two of them—exactly the same, yet so different. Literally, worlds apart.

New questions kept crowding into Logan's mind; there was so much he needed to know. Was there another Jessica on this new Earth? Would she recognize him?

The reply came instantly: *She exists. But Jessica and Logan have never met. Your strong emotional ties to your own Jessica make it imperative that you avoid contact. Keep away from her. Jessica need not concern you—and is no part of your mission.*

"How do I contact you from this new Earth?"

Contact will not be possible.

"You mean, I can't—"

We never leave this environment. We were always here. We will always be here.

The enigmatic reply failed to satisfy Logan.

"But what if I need help?"

A man named Kirov 2, who works at CenControl in Moscow, may be able to assist you in case of emergency. There is no one else.

"What about the place and time of my pickup if I succeed?"

Leave this to us. A hesitation. *There is a limitation.*

"Yes?"

We have no control over the spatial time shift that dictates the reality phase of the two planets. Eventually, these parallel worlds will cease to exist on the same cosmic plane. We cannot maintain our dual-world position indefinitely.

"How long?"

Fourteen Earthdays. If you have not exposed and destroyed the planet's power source within this period, we will be forced to abandon you.

"Impossible!" raged Logan. "It took *years* to destroy the Thinker. . . . I don't even know who or what I'm searching for!"

Fourteen days, Logan.

And a rolling, milky substance, like white smoke, began to fill the chamber. The aliens faded . . . the walls rippled . . . Logan felt himself losing consciousness.

He was on an endless chute, plunging down . . . down . . . and down. . . .

To another life.

To another Earth.

RETURN TO YESTERDAY

New California.

A full-moon summer midnight in the swarming sprawl of the Angeles Complex.

And, within the life swarm:

A glasshouse, where citizens seek voyeuristic sexual release in the rainbow-tinted night . . .

A hallucimill, dispensing dream-lifts to the jaded . . .

A nursery, with its robot-tended rows of hypnosleeping children . . .

Sleepshops, where silver darts deliver oblivion to those whose Lastday has ended . . .

DS Headquarters, a hive of black-garbed Sandmen, intent on their death-duty to the system . . .

Arcade, a fire-dazzle of blazing lights and frenzied pleasure . . .

The maze, with its swift, deep-tunnel beetle cars converging from a thousand major cities of the world . . .

And in the heart of the midnight city, in one of the glittering boxbeam lifeunits, an off-duty Sandman stirs to the sensual play of soft fingers caressing the skin of his chest. . . .

Logan awakened to the smiling female on the flowbed beside him. In the rich spill of moonlight from an open skyvent her body was flushed ivory. She wore a sheergold loverobe, accenting the peaks and hollows of her soft flesh. Her beauty was flawless.

"Remember me?" she asked in a voice of velvet. "I'm Phedra 12 . . . from Arcade." She frowned, studying his face. "You look strange. Are you lifted?"

Her question supplied Logan with an answer to mask his obvious confusion: "I took some Y-16 earlier tonight."

"Y-16?"

"New formula," Logan improvised. "Not in the 'mills yet."

She smiled again, relaxing against him, melding her body to his. "You DS have the best . . . always."

He kissed her pouting lips. "How'd you get in?"

"With this," she said, holding up a thin slotkey. "Remember? You gave it to me at the firegallery last week . . . I dance there."

Young Logan had been attracted to her, had made contact, had invited her here. . . .

"I remember now," said Logan, taking her firmly into his arms.

She was here for sex, and he'd oblige. Any other reaction would appear perverted; a young Sandman was expected to fulfill his natural urges with many women. But as Logan reached out to caress her face he flinched, jaw muscles tightening.

"What's wrong?" she asked.

His hand glowed crimson against her cheek; the time-crystal in his palm was alive again!

He smiled, shaking his head. "Nothing . . . nothing's wrong."

"It's the Y-16," she said. "Can you—I mean, are you able to—"

In answer, he tongue-kissed her deeply, fitting himself into the heated curve of her waiting body. He thrust into her, bringing a soft cat-cry from her arching throat. . . .

But as Logan made love to Phedra 12 he felt a sense of dread building darkly within him. His glowing hand was a terrible reminder of the world he thought he had escaped forever. It was back, now, all around him—as real as the cry of passion he wrung from her trembling lips. . . .

He did not sleep after Phedra left. In a loose velvrobe, he prowled the lifeunit, probing, analyzing, examining the artifacts of young Logan's life—as an ancient anthropologist might sift through the habitat of a lost tribesman.

He was trying to understand this other self, this dedicated young Sandman who homered runners with cool dispatch, who wore the death-black uniform of DS with pride, who guiltlessly helped perpetuate a system of mass murder.

Logan stared at him, at this trim-bodied young fighting machine of a man, carefully studying the sharp reflection in the wallmirror. Me, more than a decade ago. Me, still on red, well short of twenty-one, still on the hunt, still able to coldly track a fellow human, corner him, rip and unravel him with a homer. But me with something inside that cried: No!

And that was the difference.

From the beginning, in his own world, buried deep in his psyche, Logan had experienced a sense of *wrongness*; a faint, insistent pulsebeat of rebellion had existed beyond his conscious awareness. With Jessica's entry into his life that rebellion had burst forth; her love had nurtured and encouraged it. She had been the bridge that took him from Sandman to runner.

Could it happen again, here on this Earth? Could young Logan have changed, given the love of a woman like Jessica? Could he, too, have broken free of the system? From all the evidence here in this unit, and from what he already knew of this world, it seemed unlikely.

Each world was different; each man must form his own personal code of morality. Young Logan was one kind of man; he was another.

Turning his back on this reflection of a darker self, Logan walked to the plexwindow. He stood, unmoving, more than a mile above the city, watching the sun lay its thin morning fire across the eastern sky.

Then a timebird stirred the air around his head, reminding him that he must report for duty. He drew the bird from his shoulder, clicking it off; he cleared his mind, steeled himself for what lay ahead.

Time to report to DS. Time to put on the black uniform of a Sandman once more.

Time to live another man's life.

. . . A return to your yesterdays.

As the aliens had promised him it would be, this world beyond the lifeunit was an instant relive: the moving tide of young citizens, many with fear-haunted eyes (already anticipating Lastday); the black-garbed DS men, seeded darkly through the crowd, always separate from those around them (Give a Sandman space, never crowd him, keep your proper distance, he may be on the hunt!); the festive children with their flushed, excited faces, pleasure-bent and as yet untroubled by thought of Sleep; the police paravanes, hovering like predatory metal insects above the crowd, patrolling the upper levels of the Complex. All of it, painfully familiar . . .

And now the dropway, leading down to the maze platform.

Riding the car to DS Headquarters, Logan stared at his right palm, at the unblinking red glow of the flower-shaped crystal imbedded in the flesh of his hand. The aliens were brilliant; no one on Earth had ever been able to reprogram a timeflower—yet Logan's crystal was alive again, ticking off the hours of life. . . . Even for a Sandman, at twenty-one, when his palmflower blinks red-black, red-black, red-black, Lastday begins and there is no escape from Deep Sleep.

Except here, thought Logan, in *this* world, where a select few could achieve Godbirth, that mysterious ritual promising life, salvation, a higher existence.

Was it real?

When would it begin?

"Where's your Gun?"

Startled, Logan turned toward the back of the mazecar. The question had come from an eager-eyed blond youngster in a splitsleeve recsuit. He wore red hikeboots, and he smiled at Logan, obviously unafraid of Sandmen.

"I'm reporting in," said Logan. "My weapon's at DS."

"Then how come you're suited up?" asked the boy. "Off-duty Sandmen are required to wear—"

"I know the rules," cut in Logan. "So I'm bending one."

"You could be fined. It could go on your Statsheet. You could be blackmarked, and that would lower your unit average."

"You know a lot about DS."

"I'm going to be a Sandman when I'm old enough," declared the boy, eyes shining. "My name's Timson 4."

"How old are you, Timson?"

"Seven." He held up his right hand, palm out. "I just went to blue. Released from Nursery last month." He slapped his left boot. "I've already climbed the Matterhorn. Not many blues make it all the way. Three others in our group were killed trying it, and they were all older."

"Congratulations," said Logan.

"I even helped a Sandman Gun a runner! Along the Mississippi, near the Orleans Complex. He tried to get across in a small boat. I saw him steal it and I dived it and tipped the boat over. The Sandman who'd been after him used a ripper on him as he was swimming for shore. Cut him in half! The water was all red. It was exciting!"

"Why do you want to be a Sandman?"

"To kill runners. Somebody has to kill them." The boy's eyes grew cold. "They're scum. They have to die."

"For all you know, your mother might have been a runner," Logan found himself saying. "Or your father."

The boy was shocked. His face clouded with anger. "Whoever they were, they wouldn't run! Not *ever!*"

"You never know who might run," said Logan. "You get surprised sometimes."

Now the boy was staring at him with cool distrust. "Just who are you, anyway? What's your name?"

"Logan 3."

Timson's eyes popped wide.

"Have you heard of me?"

The boy gulped breath, spilling out a rapid stream of words: "You work with Francis and your killscore next to his is highest in the Complex and I'm sorry I said that about your uniform and about getting fined for breaking a rule and—" He broke off abruptly and extended a trembling hand. "Will you shake hands with me, Logan?"

Logan shook his hand. He wanted to tell this boy, Don't worship me! Don't try to become like me. Killing runners is wrong. Joining DS is wrong. The system is wrong. It will destroy you as you destroy others.

But he remained silent. Saying these things would be useless; the boy was beyond moral logic. The tapes had done their work. Timson 4 was a product of the system, as carefully manufactured as a robot, programmed to hate, to kill. Thus, Logan said nothing more as the silver car slotted into its destination platform.

He could feel the boy's eyes on him as he left the maze.

THE HIGHEST SCORE

DS Headquarters.

Unchanged, timeless, grimly austere—a windowless gray monolith rising starkly into the sky of the Angeles Complex, set apart from its surrounding buildings as a DS man is set apart from the crowd, a structure designed to strike fear into the heart of any citizen wavering between accepting Sleep or becoming a runner.

Logan mounted the steps as two men exited the building. He immediately recognized the taller: Evans 9! The childhood friend who had betrayed him at Crazy Horse, who had lured him into a deathtrap on his own world.

"Logan!" Smiling broadly, Evans walked toward him. "We were just talking about you."

The man with Evans was nervous, raw-looking, a DS trainee on the verge of Sandman status.

"This is Marak 9. I've been working with him, showing him a few things . . . learns fast . . . bright . . . you know, he's really—"

As Evans rambled on, Logan barely heard the words; in his mind, he had the image of this man at Crazy Horse, at the Thinker's Central Core, a Gun in his hand, smiling as Jonath died. . . . Logan was using all his willpower to keep from smashing his fist into Evans's face.

". . . to meet you at last . . . heard so much about you . . ."

Marak was babbling uncertain praise. Logan glared at Evans, ignoring Marak, then suddenly pushed past them into the building.

Behind him, he heard Evans shout his name in startled anger. Then the heavy DS entrance door slid closed, cutting off the sound.

Just inside, Logan paused, drew a long breath— telling himself, fiercely, that he must *never* react this way again, that he must rigorously keep the two worlds separate in his mind. He must never allow emotions relating to *his* world to dictate present behavior in this one. If you do, you'll ruin it all, he warned himself, you'll lose Godbirth, lose your chance to succeed in this mission, lose Jess and Jaq forever. Damn you, never again! *Never!*

And, breathing deeply, he moved toward the readyroom.

It was crowded with DS on shiftchange, suiting up for duty. Already uniformed, Logan had only to check out a Follower and an ammopac. As he did this, his name was called by the talkboard. Message for him.

"Logan 3," he said, facing the board, "Message?"

"From Francis," the board told him. "Waiting in the Huntarea. You are to join him there."

"Acknowledged," Logan said.

He faced a challenge. Logan was standing before the Gunwall at the end of the weapons corridor. If the skin-pattern alterations on his palm were less than perfect, an alarm would sound the moment he touched the wall—and before he could attempt an explanation he'd be Gunned to ash.

"Identity," repeated the metallic voice. It had already challenged him once; Logan knew he *must* respond.

He pressed the palm of his left hand firmly into the wall's identiplate. No alarm! Accepted.

A panel gleamed back to reveal the Gun, nested in its black-velvet alcove.

But the challenge was not over. Now, another

critical stage. The alteration on his palm had been properly matched to young Logan's—but if the more complex pore configuration on his thumb and fingers was even microscopically incorrect, the Gun would detonate upon skin contact, since each DS weapon was pore-coded to the individual operative to whom it was issued.

Logan could feel the sweat beading his upper lip as he slowly reached in to curl his fingers around the cool pearl handle of the Gun. . . .

Full contact. Perfect.

The corridor lights glinted along the dark blue barrel as Logan checked the weapon for full load: tangler, ripper, needler, nitro, vapor—and the deadly, body-tracking, nerve-destroying homer.

There was no denying the power of the Gun. Logan had fought his way to the Keys with such a weapon; he had used a Sandman's Gun to win back Jessica from the Borgia Riders. Now he felt the power radiating through his fingers and arm, firing his flesh.

Power and killing force.

To use as chosen—for good or for evil.

Logan had never liked simkill workouts in the Huntarea, but they were required for all DS, designed (as the manual phrased it) "to tune the reflexes and sharpen an operative's reaction time to situations not normally encountered in the course of a standard outside hunt."

Francis held the highest simkill score at Angeles. All his simulated kills were clean; he never wounded. He was deadly accurate at almost any range, no matter how difficult the situation or the terrain. Francis was exactly what his record indicated: the ideal DS operative—keen-minded, inventive, emotionless, precise. Francis did not make mistakes, and when a runner made one, he was there, a tireless force, to take advantage of it, of any weakness.

And eventually, Logan thought, I must kill him, just as the aliens said. He will have to be stopped.

But not today. No, today I'll hunt with him,

match my skill against his, giving him no reason to mistrust me.

Because, at this moment, to Logan, Francis was the most important man alive on this death-haunted planet.

Logan crossed the yard, a reserve area for DS trainees. A dozen of them, wearing opaque head-shields, were engaged in Blind Combat, led by a flat-faced instructor who displayed open disgust as he slammed one young trainee after another into the dirt.

"Concentrate!" he lashed at them. "Determine my approach angle from the sound of my boots. Runner at night won't give you warning. Cut your throat from behind. Strangle on your own blood! No second chance then—so concentrate *now!"*

As he watched, Logan was suddenly aware of a faint scraping sound behind him, but before he could turn he was dumped into the yard, belly down.

A dry chuckle above him. "Concentrate, Logan, concentrate!"

"Damn you, Francis!"

Logan stood up, brushing sand from his tunic. He glared at the tall, thin man in black. The eyes were darker than midnight, mocking and steady in the narrow, lean-cheeked face. These eyes missed nothing. Unblinking, penetrating, they measured Logan with a glint of cold humor.

"You're not going to score so well today if you don't sharpen up," said Francis as they began walking toward the Huntarea. "You might have figured I'd try for a bodythrow. You know me well enough."

"Yes," said Logan tightly, "I know you." Then he forced a lighter tone into his voice. "You *do* enjoy your little games."

"Not a game," said the tall man. His dark eyes were serious. "If I'd been a runner you might be dead right now."

"But I'm alive," said Logan flatly. "And I can handle runners. I do it well."

"I do it better," wolf-grinned Francis. "I always have."

The smug projection of superiority from Francis steeled Logan, made him determined to excel in their area workout. He was supremely skilled with a Gun, was a master of body combat, and refused to be intimidated by his rival's vaunted prowess.

Silently, each wholly intent on the trials to come, they traversed a long, brightly illumined slot tunnel and emerged into the main hunt arena.

Covering several square miles, the entire area had been constructed under a vast glasite dome in which every type and degree of weather could be expertly simulated; here, too, all combat conditions, however rigorous, could be duplicated.

The test ground was split into two branching sections. One route led right, twisting through spiked brushweed and snaretraps; the second route snaked left, across a man-made swamp. The terrain in both was equally treacherous, and the android runners were equally dangerous. No DS man had been killed in a workout, but injuries were common, some of them severe. Logan could not afford to be seriously injured; it might delay Godbirth—and there must be no delays.

They stood at the crossway.

"Your choice," said Francis. "Right or left."

"Left," said Logan.

"See you on the other side." Francis grinned, moving swiftly for the high brush.

Logan felt confident as he set off along the left attack trail. The DS Huntarea in his world was very similar, yet familiarity was not a factor in this contest. There was no way to anticipate what lay ahead, since each route was regularly reprogrammed. You never knew when sudden fog might blind you, or when an artificial sun would dazzle blindingly from the domed sky, or when thick darkness might descend to throw you off balance, make you vulnerable. . . .

The first attack came with shocking swiftness: a male android runner, dropping from a tree onto Logan's back. He had a buzzblade, and if he could drive the blade into Logan's body in a vital flesh area Logan's "kill" would be reversed. No skin penetration, no blood, but the contact point would be registered. For

Logan, a negative encounter. Each negative encounter would cancel three simkills on the final score.

But Logan easily loop-rolled the runner over his shoulder and broke the robot's neck with a single down-chopping blow. Simkill: score 1.

Four hours of this.

Miles of swamp and jungle, of quicksand and rockslides, of chilling rain gusts, blast-furnace heat, savage winds. . . . And always the cleverly programmed robot runners attacking from ambush, armed and dangerous. You could never relax; you were never beyond assault. Absolute concentration was required.

Concentrate! Logan told himself when a female almost got him with a chokewire. He'd allowed her to come up behind him from a blind in the rocks, and the wire was around his neck before he managed a whipspin that sent her sprawling. Francis was right: concentration was the key. Lose that cutting edge of alertness and the hunter becomes the victim.

Four hours . . . and finally it was over.

Francis, looking cool and unwinded, boots glistening, his uniform dusted, was already at the final crossway when Logan arrived.

Logan's uniform was torn in several places; his tunic was mud-splattered ripped at the shoulder. He came in limping, favoring his right foot.

"Sandtrap?" Francis asked casually. An amused smile played at his lips.

"Stunrod," said Logan, sitting down wearily. "Didn't know androids carried the things!"

The tall man shook his head. "Whatever a runner could have, or steal, the robots get. Is it bad?"

Logan slipped off his right boot; the lower leg was blue and swollen. "Bad enough."

"Santini can fix it."

Logan looked blank.

"New body tech at the gym. Let him work the leg. You'll be fine."

"I'll try him," said Logan, wincing as he tabbed the boot closed. He stood up, testing his weight. At least he could still hobble. The rod had caught him just below the knee and his leg had collapsed under him.

He'd managed to fire as he fell, gutting the robot with a nitro. But it had been close—and painful.

Logan looked at Francis. "Well . . . shall we?"

The tall man grinned. "Are you sure you want the bad news—a poor crip' like you?"

"Score it," snapped Logan.

Francis palmed the scorepanel. A crimson number blazed to life on the board: 22.

"Hey," said Francis softly. "Two up from my last workout. That's a sweet total." He looked at Logan with amused eyes. "Your turn, friend."

Logan palmed the wall and the simkill score flashed red: 24.

Francis stared at it, his grin fading. He let out a soft breath. "Well, well . . ."

"My right leg slowed me over the last mile," said Logan. "But it's not a bad total."

Francis flipped aside the vitabar he'd been chewing and moved sullenly through the slipexit.

Logan followed. His leg felt better already.

For the first time that day, he was smiling.

THE LAST HUNT

Santini 14 had always been unique. In Nursery, long after midnight, while the other children were in their slotbeds, hypnotapes whispering to them as they slept, young Santini 14 was in the romproom, challenging the musclebelts, or working the jumpbars, or twisting through the intricate network of whipchutes—toughening himself, shaping his body as a sculptor shapes fireglass, gaining mastery over bone and muscle.

On blue, clear of the nurseries, he used his

freetime to visit all of the world's prime bodybuild cen-
ters—and on red, just past fifteen, he had opened his
own bodyshop. His enlistment with DS, at Angeles
Complex, was inevitable.

Due to the odd irregularities of the twin Earths,
Santini had never existed in Logan's world. Therefore,
his talent was *truly* unique.

Logan had expected the usual swirlnerve treatment, but Santini employed a personal method of vi-
bromassage, producing immediate relief. The swelling
vanished and the discoloration was replaced by healthy
skin tone.

"Up!" ordered Santini, clapping his hands.
"Jump, Sandman! Leap! Kick! You're perfect."

Logan eased off the table, tried some knee bends,
placing full weight on his right leg. He was astonished.
No pain. No muscle pull or discomfort.

"Perfect." Logan nodded. "Thanks!"

Santini smiled lazily and moved closer. "The body
holds many secrets. Mysteries of the flesh. I track them
down as you track down runners." Closer to Logan,
the smile softened. "I'd say we are very much the
same, you and I. What would you say?"

And he stroked Logan's upper arm with slow fingers.

Logan stepped away. "I'd say the treatment is
over."

Francis met him outside the gym, in a state of ela-
tion. His face was flushed and his dark eyes danced
with energy.

"It's here, Logan." He closed the fingers of his
left hand into a fist. "It's ours!"

"What are you talking about?"

"Godbirth!"

Logan's heart trip-hammered at the word; he felt
a surge of pure triumph. *Godbirth!* The gate back to
Jess and Jaq . . .

"Is it confirmed?"

"Will be by tonight," said Francis. "That's when
we'll be officially notified by the computer. I got advance word, straight off the report line."

"What about our duty status?"

"We're up for one last hunt," said Francis. "Then it's freetime to Godbirth—time to do whatever we want, anywhere."

"For how long?"

"Ten days. Then we'll be taken to the Place of Miracles."

"I didn't expect it this soon," Logan admitted.

The gaunt man clapped Logan's shoulder. "Means we reach Nirvana. No Sleep for *us* at twenty-one! We're joining the Gods. We'll live forever!"

Logan had a multitude of questions he dared not ask. What was Nirvana? Who were the Gods? Where was the Place of Miracles? Was Godbirth *literal* immortality? What did it involve?

Even more confusing: Why didn't the aliens already have these answers? They seemed to know so much about details on this alternate Earth—but nothing of its central ritual.

Why?

Why?

The report room: an ultrasophisticated nerve center for DS, the tracking and dispatch area from which a tide of black-clad operatives flowed out into the arteries of the southwest.

Facing this coldly efficient meld of man and machine, designed to eliminate human life, the past was depressingly alive for Logan. Without Argos, without Ballard, without a Sanctuary Line, it seemed impossible that any runner, however tenacious and resourceful, could escape this deadly electronic net. Indeed, on this world, the goal of outrunning the Gun was a dream turned nightmare. Hope without substance. On this Earth, Logan knew, he'd have had no chance.

Francis touched his arm. "I've got our man on the board," he said, speaking above the hive-hum of activity.

Logan nodded.

"He blacked at 0800, took over a police paravane, but didn't get far in it. Crashed near Indio.

Right now he's on the desert, somewhere between Palm Springs and Indian Wells."

"Armed?" asked Logan, as they moved to the scanwall.

"Fuser," said Francis. "Got it with the paravane. Hasn't killed anybody with it yet, but he's likely to if someone tries to stop him. We'll have to be careful." A thin smile. "Last hunt, old friend. Let's do it right."

Logan was realistic enough to know that this runner would have to die. Short of destroying Francis, there was no way for him to save the man's life. And even if he did kill Francis to save him, another DS man would homer him. No, there was nothing he could do to help the doomed runner.

But at least, he vowed to himself, *I* won't make the kill. The final score will go to Francis.

Behind Logan's thoughts, Francis was filling in the runner's history: "Escaped a state nursery in Kansas City when he was six. Arrested at ten for printing anti-Sleep material. Which cost him six months in a work compound. At sixteen, blocked a DS man on a hunt. Nineteen to twenty—pairups with at least two known subversives."

"Real misfit." Logan nodded. "Guess he doesn't like the system much."

"We've been watching him," said a board tech. "Stayed with his sister at a quad in the Beverly sector for a while. We figured he'd run on black. Took us by surprise, though, when he grabbed that paravane. This boy's smart. Smart and dangerous."

Francis grinned. "That's how I like 'em." He looked at Logan. "This last one might be fun after all."

"Maybe," said Logan.

The board tech punched in the scan coordinates.

Logan was stunned as the runner's tri-dimensional image filled the scanboard: it was Doyle!

Jessica's brother!

Data quick-flashed across the screen:

Runner . . . DOYLE 10-14302
Height . . . 6–1
Weight . . . 180

Hair . . . DARK BROWN

Eyes . . . SAME

Physical markings . . . SMALL SCAR ABOVE RIGHT
                                  EYE

DS status . . . CRYSTAL BLACKED 0800 . . . ARCADE

Present location . . . DESERT AREA . . . PALM
                                  SPRINGS . . .

Scope reading . . . NEGATIVE

WARNING . . . WARNING . . . WARNING . . .
          WARNING . . . WARNING
APPROACH WITH CAUTION . . . SUBJECT
ARMED WITH STOLEN X-9Z FUSE WEAPON

"Are you all right?" Francis was staring at him.

Logan had unconsciously fisted both hands; his knuckles were white, his face taut with suppressed emotion. He nodded slowly.

"Something's wrong."

"It's just that he—looks like a man I knew."

"Friend?"

"No . . . just someone I knew once."

"Well, we'd better move on this one. They're holding a car for us." Francis checked his Follower. "They tried for a scope reading. No go. But we can lock into him once we hit the desert."

"Yes, we can do that," said Logan. His tone was flat and mechanical. He was numbed by the realization that it was happening all over again; he was being forced to hunt down Jessica's brother here on this Earth exactly as he had done in the past, on his own world.

"The board tech mentioned he'd been staying with a sister," Logan said as they took a dropchute to the DS platform. "Know anything about her?"

"A little," said Francis. "Name's Jessica 6. No arrest history. Seems stable enough, but with a brother like Doyle you can never tell."

"She on red?"

"Right . . . due for Sleep anytime now. When she blacks they'll be watching her."

On the maze platform they boarded the waiting

express vehicle. The canopy slid closed and the mazecar moved out, rapidly gaining tunnel speed.

The Indio platform, just over two hundred miles from DS Headquarters, was less than a minute's ride.

They emerged into the dry windless heat of a desert afternoon, into a smell of baked sand, of sun-seared rock and cactus.

Francis squinted at the hot blue sky. A vulture rode the upper air currents in a long, lazy patrol.

"He's hunting, too," said Francis with a thin smile. "I figure we'll have better luck!"

A DS hovercat was waiting for them beyond the platform, glinting silver-blue in the shimmering heat. This rugged little machine could navigate any type of desert terrain. Solar-powered, its metalloid skin was impervious to assault by any hand weapon; a Fuser charge, exploding along its surface, would leave no trace. And the cat was fast.

Francis popped the jumpdoor and they climbed inside.

"We should be able to get a fix on him," said Francis, working the cat's trackscreen. "He can't be too far."

Logan was thinking of the other Doyle—of how he'd had the man in direct kill range but had not fired. It was the first time Logan had ever done such a thing, failing to use the Gun. It was the crack in his DS armor, the real beginning of his run for Sanctuary. In that earlier hunt, Doyle had died in Cathedral; the cubs had ripped him apart. But *we* were responsible, thought Logan; he was running from *us* when the cubs got him.

How Jess had hated him for her brother's death! Yet, without Doyle, he'd never have known her . . . loved her . . . fought to keep her. . . .

"Ah, *there's* our boy!" The triumphant voice of Francis erased Logan's thoughts. He glanced at the readout: a green dot was inching across the screen like a tiny electronic insect.

"I make him about five miles this side of Indian

Wells," said Francis. "We'll come in through Spiker Wash. That'll put us right on him."

"What's he trying to do?"

"Stay alive." Francis grinned, engaging power. The cat hissed over the sand. "Maybe he figures to pick up a vehicle at the Wells." Francis leaned back; his Gun was unholstered, and he smoothed long fingers over its cool pearl handle. "All he'll pick up is a homer."

Something was coming.

Something tall and dark and powerful.

In the close heat of the rocks, the scorpion was motionless, sensing danger, tail raised to strike. It was female, had recently given birth to its young, and carried them in a brood pouch, carefully guarded. It would kill to survive.

A shadow crossed the rock. The scorpion tensed. A heavy boot heel smashed down, ending its life.

Doyle hated scorpions. As a boy, on this same desert, he'd been hit by one and had almost died of the virulent poison. Yet, basically, he respected them, as he respected the rattler and the lizard, as he respected all living things that fight back.

The desert itself he loved. It had always fascinated him with its paradoxes, its odd character, its subtle beauty. For Doyle 10, the desert retained its purity. It defied man's corruption. It was Doyle's private ocean—an easy-rolling sea of sand and rock and cactus, of smokewood and manzanita—and it was only natural, at the end, that he should return here. And this *was* the end for him. He knew it, accepted it. They were coming for him. His death lay in their Guns as a pearl in an oyster. The homer would find him. No rock could shelter him against it.

And what if he *did* reach the Wells? What if he *could* use the hoverstick he'd hidden there? The sky would not shelter him. He could not escape DS. Not on the ground, nor in the air, nor on the sea. The men of Deep Sleep would find him and destroy him for his terrible crime of refusing to accept death at twenty-one. What good was running?

Yet Doyle ran.

Under the sun-blazed sky, through thorn-spiked dry washes, along wind-eroded gullies, over baked clusters of rock and cactus, his lips puffed and bleeding, his clothing in tatters, hands broken-skinned and swollen—fighting to stay alive another hour, another minute, knowing he must die and crying *I'll live!* . . . knowing he must lose and crying *I'll win!* . . . running until he dropped heavily to his knees in the dry hot sand, until the breath in his lungs was fire, until he heard the buzzing whir of a hovercat that was . . .

Death.

"That's him!" shouted Francis, stopping the cat. "On his knees over there near the rocks." The harsh chuckle, the Gun in his hand. "Maybe he's praying to us, Logan! We'll soon be Gods . . . maybe he knows!"

"He's just exhausted," said Logan quietly. "He can't go on, is all."

"I was hoping he'd give us a fight, maybe try using that Fuser of his. Liven things up. After all, it's our last hunt." He sighed. "Too easy. Too damned easy."

Logan reluctantly left the sandcat, following Francis, his weapon still holstered. He didn't trust himself with it, not at this moment. He might just Gun Francis here and now, because the thought of his DS partner sending a homer blistering into that poor kneeling wretch was almost more than Logan could stand.

"You want the shot?" asked Francis as Logan moved up beside him.

"No, it's yours, Francis. . . . Your last official kill." It was difficult to keep the bitterness from his voice.

"Fair enough, old friend." The gaunt man nodded. "I was just being generous."

Doyle pulled himself to his feet gasping, blood and salt sweat in his eyes. He rubbed at them. They wouldn't focus properly on the two advancing figures—heat-rippled shapes of black moving toward him across the hot sand.

The shapes had stopped. Something one of them held caught the sun, dazzling his eyes. Doyle blinked, squinted, trying to get it in focus.

Gun.

That's what it was. He's going to do it, Doyle. Oh, yes, he'll do it. He'll fire the homer at you and the thing will find you and the pain will be unbelievable and your flesh will burst and your nerves will fry and your body explode in bands of pain. . . .

Don't let him do it to you, Doyle. Don't let him. Don't.

"What's he doing?" asked Francis, bringing up the Gun.

Logan watched the man. "Inside his shirt. He's—"

"Fuser!" shouted Francis, dropping hard into the sand, pulling Logan down with him. The tall man's face was eager; sparks lived in his flat dark eyes. "By God, he's going to make a fight of it after all!"

But Francis was wrong.

One harsh sizzle of heat and Doyle toppled backward into the rocks, hands splayed, head a charred husk on his neck.

The Fuser fell into the sand.

"Used it on himself," said Logan.

The two men walked over to him and looked down at the lifeless body. The flies were already at it.

"Damn," said Francis softly.

ONE MORE TIME

Standing by the Gunwall, at the end of the long gray corridor at DS, Logan unsnapped his holster and drew out the silver-barreled weapon. He weighed it in his hands.

The wall was waiting.

Every Sandman, at duty's end, was required to return his Gun. No exceptions. In *his* world, Logan had broken that rule, had taken a Gun with him when he ran—but here such an act was impossible.

In destroying the power behind Godbirth, he could well use such a potent weapon, but he knew he must accomplish his mission without it.

Logan replaced the weapon, snugging the heavy Gun back into its velvet wallnest. The panel closed. The Gun was no longer his.

At least he hadn't been forced to use it on Doyle.

Francis was waiting on the steps that night when Logan exited DS Headquarters. Both wore citizen casuals. They had checked their uniforms and equipment and had filed their reports and now were free of duty. Free. A strange word in this world, thought Logan, a perversion of meaning. No one on this Earth was free.

Francis was in high spirits. "What about celebrating? I've got some Volney's at my unit. Vintage stuff. And we can find girls in Arcade—make a night of it."

The Francis whom Logan had known never celebrated anything; usually it was Logan who asked his dour friend to party. The answer had always been

37

no. Now the situation was reversed: Logan declined the offer.

"But why? By morning we'll have our official notification. This is a special occasion, Logan—a *very* special occasion!"

Logan smiled. "It's been a long day," he said. "Leg's still bothering me some. I need to ease off, be alone."

"All right, friend," said Francis. "But I leave early tomorrow on freetime. Want to get in some diving—so I won't be seeing you for a while."

Logan was suddenly concerned. "Where do we meet? For Godbirth, I mean."

"Thought you knew. Back here at DS, in exactly ten days. We leave from here with the others. The Chosen Ones."

"I'll be here." Logan nodded.

"In case you need to reach me," said the tall man, "here's my faxcode number. My unit will know where I am."

He handed a foilcard to Logan. "Happy freetime!"

"You too," said Logan.

"Ten days," said Francis, and walked off, whistling, into the darkness.

From the moment Doyle's image had materialized on the scanscreen, Logan knew that nothing could stop him from seeing Jessica. It would be a major risk. The aliens had specifically warned him not to attempt contact with her—and, because of her brother, she was on DS lists as a "possible subversive."

Thus, Logan had strong reasons for avoiding her, and he experienced self-anger at the risk he was taking. Just a week and a half from Godbirth and he was acting like the worst kind of fool.

But he couldn't stop himself.

He had checked Doyle's faxfile before leaving DS and had found Jessica's unit number—and now he was in a mazecar heading for the Beverly sector.

He rationalized the action. If DS did discover his visit, he could classify it under duty routine. As a prime hunter involved in her brother's death, he had the right to notify Jessica. This was often done by Sandmen. A civic obligation. He could even strengthen his position by telling DS that since Jessica 6 was of doubtful status, he had decided to check her out, unofficially, for possible subversive activity.

Routine.

He just wanted to meet her, that was all. A brief meeting to satisfy his emotional desire to see her face, hear her voice. . . .

Just one brief meeting.

The mazecar slotted into the Beverly platform and Logan rode a lifebelt to the street level.

This sector, built over the old, moneyed Beverly Hills–Bel-Air–Brentwood area, was a hub for merchantmen specializing in ultraluxury. Here, one could order custom-designed hovercraft for street and sky, or body jewels coded to the purchaser's individual skin chemistry, or bizarre robotic pets of all types (Take home a Tigon, half-tiger, half-lion! Buy yourself a Monkeybird!), or tri-dimensional home consoles programmed for total mythic/historic owner participation (Dance with Valentino! Make love to Cleopatra! Match swords with Morgan the Pirate!).

Logan moved past the richly textured shops— pausing at one of them, a jewelmaker's window. Displayed inside, a flame-blue throatclasp, delicately sculpted and overlaid with silver filigree. . . .

Jess had worn one exactly like it! Identical to the clasp he'd taken to old Andar on the Bridge. He stared at it for a long moment, remembering. . . .

And walked on.

Reaching Jessica's quadunit, Logan hesitated outside the entrance. One last chance to turn back, he told himself. One last chance to place reason and logic above emotion.

Don't go in, Logan!

He entered the building.

A hibelt took him to the third level, and although it was only a short walk to unit 3-11, the wide copper corridor seemed endless to Logan. He could barely contain his nervous excitement as he reached Jessica's door.

The heat of his body activated the unit scanner. He waited.

Was she out? Or was she inside, peering at him through the scanner? Would she answer?

Then: "What is it you want?"

Her voice, reaching out into the corridor, the voice of the woman he loved, the mother of his new child. The voice, unmistakably Jessica's. But, of course, not hers at all.

"I—have news of your brother."

The door instantly petaled back, and she was there.

"Come in."

Numbly, Logan followed her into the unit.

The *same!* Everything the same: hands, eyes, lips . . . the way she cants her head a bit to the left as she walks . . . the suppleness of her body . . . the dark hair flowing along her back . . . even the splitsleeve robe she wore; Jess had one just like it!

Jess! Oh, Jess!

"I know you," she said, turning to face him, her eyes clear and steady on his. "You're Logan."

Her words stunned him. How *could* she know him? The aliens had told him that in this world the two of them had never met.

"Don't look so surprised," she said, smiling. "You're famous . . . the famous Logan 3, a DS Gunmaster . . . Sandman with a top killscore. I've seen you on the tri-dims—but I never thought I'd have a chance to really meet you."

She nodded toward a foamchair near the window of the small neatly arranged unit. "Please . . . relax. Can I get you anything?"

Logan settled into the chair, thrown off balance by her casualness. Chatting about tri-dims, offering me a drink—when I've just seen her brother die. She doesn't know that, of course. Still, I said I had news of him, and she may well suspect that he turned runner. Why isn't she questioning me about him?

Jessica repeated her offer, and he nodded. Actually, he could use a drink. Steady him down. "Some Irish—if you have it."

"Black Irish it is," she said, smiling. "And I'll have one with you."

She dialed the wall, received the two drinks, gave him one, then sat down on a flowcouch next to him. Calm and casual.

"Now . . . about my brother. You have news of Doyle?"

"Yes," he said, hesitating. "I thought I should—"

"He's dead, isn't he?" she asked flatly.

"Yes," said Logan.

"Doyle told me he was going to run," she said, her tone devoid of shock or sadness. She looked steadily at Logan and asked without emotion, "Did you kill him?"

"No, but I was part of the team that hunted him," said Logan. "It was suicide. He'd taken a Fuser . . . and when he saw us coming—"

"Us?"

"Francis was on the hunt with me. We usually team together."

"I know," she said, leaning back into the couch to sip the whiskey. "I've heard of Francis. He's very efficient."

"Very," said Logan.

"Doyle was always such a fool. I told him not to run. Told him he had no chance. But, being a fool, he ran. He was like that. You could never talk sense to Doyle."

Cold, thought Logan, totally unmoved by her brother's death. She may *look* exactly like Jess, but this is another breed of cat. This woman has nothing of her tenderness, her compassion, her sensitivity. . . .

Logan finished his drink and stood up. "Well, I'd better go. I just wanted you to know about your brother."

"Listen," she said, walking him to the door, "we're having a quad party tomorrow night. In Arcade, at the Hastings gallery. Care to come?"

He stared at her. How could she? With her brother dead—a party!

"Sorry," he said.

She put her hand lightly on his arm, and her touch was electric, startling. "Oh, *do* come, Logan. You'll have fun, I promise!"

She smiled at him radiantly. *Jessica's* smile.

And he found himself asking: "What time?"

She gave him a time and a location and he said yes, he'd be there, and she smiled again and he left the unit asking himself, *why?* Why did I agree to go? What possessed me to say I'd go?

She did. Jessica possessed you. You want to see her again. You *must* see her again. Despite everything. Despite the stupidity of it, the risk of it.

In the maze, as the car swept through tunneled night, Logan saw her in his mind, clear and sharp and lovely.

She's not like you at all, Jess . . . but she *is* you, the only you I've got in this world. I could never love her as I love you. I don't even *like* her. But I'm drawn to her. A moth to flame.

One more time.

I'll see her one more time.

A GOOD CITIZEN

The Central Computer, at Angeles Complex, was housed in a mile-high tower of sunglass, its outer surface covered with an unending mosaic depicting the history of man from the earliest known records, millions of years ago, to the present age. The work had taken two decades to complete, and symbolized the computer's stored knowledge, the repository of man's wisdom, the sources from which each citizen of the

Complex could partake—a great river of facts, images, and history, which flowed through Cencomp to feed the masses.

After his meeting with Jess, Logan spent most of the following day at Cencomp—determined to learn all he could about the upcoming ritual he was to undergo with Francis. He drew a complete blank.

Nothing about Godbirth.

Nothing about the Place of Miracles.

Nothing about Nirvana.

No faxsheets, statrecords, readouts, history tapes.

Nothing.

And when he questioned the computer as to why, he was told that such data was nonexistent.

"But it *must* exist!" argued Logan. "Godbirth exists!"

"The data you request is nonexistent," repeated the soft, neutered voice of Cencomp.

"What about all the Sandmen who have been selected for Godbirth?"

"They are nonexistent."

"The place of Miracles?"

"Nonexistent."

"Nirvana?"

"Nonexistent."

"The Gods!"

"Nonexistent."

Logan sat in the padded Questionchair, staring at the featureless computerwall. A tiny, glowing voicecylinder halfway between floor and ceiling was the only visual contact with the immense powerhouse of stored data behind the wall.

He felt helpless, frustrated. And angry.

"I received official comp-notification of acceptance for Godbirth," Logan said, keeping his tone level. A display of temper would achieve nothing; displayed emotion brought no profit here.

"That is correct. You received notification."

Logan leaned forward, boring in. Logic. The computer could not refute logic. "How can I receive notification of a ritual that does not exist? Please explain that."

"It is not possible to render explanations relating to nonexistent data," said the calm computer-voice.

"But the notification exists!"

"The notification exists. That is correct. But the data relating to it is nonexistent."

"But if you admit sending me a—" Logan sighed, letting the sentence die.

"Your question is unclear. Please clarify or I cannot offer you a reply."

"Never mind," said Logan. "The question is canceled."

No wonder Francis didn't say much to him about Godbirth. Logan had assumed that Francis knew a great deal about the ritual, but obviously that assumption was incorrect.

He stood up to leave.

"We hope you have gained wisdom and satisfaction from your visit with us," said the computer-voice. "Our services are always available to you, and you are always free to ask whatever questions may—"

It was still talking as Logan muttered an obscenity and left the chamber.

He had gained nothing here but frustration.

The dancer moved with hypnotic grace, weaving sinuous flame patterns through the crowd, creating a body-symphony in rippled yellow fire.

Logan inhaled her sharply erotic fragrance, released as flames slowly consumed the potent skin cosmetic she wore.

"Striking, isn't she?" asked Jessica, sitting close to him in the fiery dark.

"Yes, she's that, all right," agreed Logan, watching the dancer weave a flame ring around their table. Her smile dazzled through a halo of fire-blazed blue.

"She seems to know you."

He nodded. "She's Phedra 12. We've had sex."

"She must be a marvelous lover," said Jessica. "Such exquisite body control."

Logan said nothing to this.

They were in the Hastings firegallery, and the par-

tygoers around them were having a fine time, proud of
netting the famous Logan 3 for their group. Society
status symbol. Instant celebrity prize.

As Phedra danced away, deeper into the crowd,
Jessica leaned close to Logan. Her eyes appraised him
coolly. "You're not enjoying yourself much, are you?"

"I shouldn't be here."

"Tell me why. Don't you like me?" She pressed
her right leg against his. "I thought you liked me."

Logan failed to respond. Jessica's blatant sexuality
sickened him. He'd hunted down her brother and
should be held responsible, in her eyes, for Doyle's violent death. Yet here she was, in a daring fullslash par-
tysuit, preening to him, soliciting his lust, totally cold
to what had happened to her brother. In a perverse
sense, his part in Doyle's death seemed to make him
more attractive to her.

It was all wrong. Distorted.

Coming here tonight had been painful for Logan.
Moving through the pleasure-gorged crowds of Arcade,
assaulted by the mad cacophony of lights and sounds
and colors, he was struck anew by the horrible emp-
tiness of it all. Pleasure now, and death waiting beyond
the lights.

For Logan, Arcade encapsulated the basic
sickness of this society—just as it had in his own world
prior to the final destruction of the Thinker. Pleasure
without freedom. Pleasure without hope. A mockery.
A lure to dull the mind, to lead the citizen into
Sleep . . .

"I'd better leave," said Logan. "I'm not much
good at parties."

Jessica stood up. "All right, I'll go too. Will you
take me back to my unit?"

Suddenly, abruptly, they moved together and she
was in his arms. The clean scent of her shining hair
reached him, the subtle perfume of her skin. . . . With
soft fingers, she touched his face, leaned to kiss him,
her lips fierce and hot on his.

In Jessica's lifeunit, totally lost in one another's
flesh, they made love into the dawn. Then, sated, they

slept, skin to skin, as the morning sun tinted the sky
over Angeles Complex in soft pastels.

Logan woke first, slipped quietly from the
flowbed, dressed, and exited the unit.

On a pillow next to the sleeping woman he left a
note:

> Jessica:
> I won't see you again. Don't
> try to contact me. This is over.
> **L.**

And in the mazecar, heading back to his sector,
he did not regret the harshness of the note. He knew
that what he had done was perverted—making love to
this woman while his own Jess, waiting with child, was
lost to him across space on another world.

He would end this madness here and now. He
should never have given in to his initial compulsion,
should never have gone to see this second Jessica.
Their lovemaking, however passionate, was a distortion
of his love for Jess, and he was disgusted with his self-
weakness.

Over. Done.
Ended.

When Logan walked into his lifeunit, three tall
police officers were waiting for him, their bright lemon-
colored tunics contrasting with the dark solemnity of
their faces.

"I'm Bracker—Federal Branch," said the tallest
of them. His eyes were slate-colored, his thin lips un-
smiling. "Are you Logan 3—1639?"

"You know I am." Logan met his measured gaze.
"What do you want with me?"

"We have reason to believe that you are in viola-
tion of a prime citystate law," said the policeman.

"What law?"

"Possession and dissemination of a highly toxic
and illegal substance."

"You'd better leave," said Logan tightly. "I'm
with DS. We have immunity against this sort of harass-
ment."

"DS immunity does not apply in this case," said Bracker.

"Who sent you here?"

"Never mind that. We're here."

Logan expelled angry breath. "I'd like to know the nature of this 'highly toxic' substance."

Bracker raised a finger—and one of his men dipped a hand into the upper pocket of Logan's zipjacket, extracting a small, wafer-thin white disc.

"DD-15," said Bracker, holding up the disc. "Unofficially known as Death Dust."

Logan was quite familiar with this drug. DD-15 was used exclusively in Medlab control work and was strictly forbidden to citizens, including DS operatives. It was potent and deadly.

"That's not mine," said Logan calmly. "It does not belong to me, and I have absolutely no idea where it came from."

"Naturally," said Bracker, smiling faintly. He nodded to the others. "Take him."

Logan did not resist. His hands were tapewired behind him, and he was led from the unit directly to a waiting police paravane outside the building.

The ride to Federal Headquarters was swift and silent.

The interrogation room smelled of fear. The air was hot and close. No vents or windows. The sour fearsweat of numberless accused citizens lingered here; it permeated the pores of the room, creating an oppressive atmosphere designed to inspire breakdown and confession.

Logan, in a holdchair, faced Bracker and his men—just as he had faced the aliens in the giant mothership. And with the same sense of helplessness. How could he prove his innocence? Someone had planted the Dust on him. Someone who wanted to hurt him, to place him in severe jeopardy. Someone.

Phedra 12.

She stood in the room's open doorway, wearing a loose dun-brown monksrobe that obscured the extravagant curves of her body. Her face was scrubbed of makeup; she looked much younger, almost childlike. And there was mock sadness in her usually sensual eyes.

"I hate doing this to you, Logan, really I do," she said in a small, apologetic voice. "But I'm a good citizen. I've always been loyal to the system. I just couldn't let you do it."

"And what did I do, Phedra?" Logan asked.

"That stuff you were using . . . passing around . . . that awful stuff!" She shuddered.

"This is the man you saw in Arcade?" asked Bracker.

"Yes." She nodded. "Logan 3. He's famous. Everyone knows him. Before he began using . . . the drug . . . I was happy to be there, *proud* to dance for him."

"She's jealous," Logan snapped to the others in the room. He swung his eyes to hers, glaring. "Because I was with another woman. That's why you're doing this. Tell them the truth. *Admit* it!"

"No—I can't lie for you, Logan. Don't ask me to lie!" And she lowered her eyes, seemingly on the verge of tears.

A class act, thought Logan. First class all the way.

Bracker walked close to her. "The woman he was with," prompted the tall officer. "Tell us her name." He smiled thinly. "For the record."

"Jessica 6," said Phedra softly.

"Right." Bracker nodded. His voice hardened: "Bring her in."

And Jessica was suddenly there in the room with Logan, looking stunned and shaken. Bracker led her to a holdchair and she sat down, a glazed expression on her face.

"I don't understand," she said. "Why am I here?"

"Tell her why, Logan." Bracker smiled. "She shared the fun at Arcade. Now she's sharing this. Tell her why she's here."

"It's Phedra," said Logan bitterly. "She's been lying, trying to—"

"That's the woman! That's her!" said Phedra,

overriding his words, pointing at Jessica. "She was there with him."

"And was she also using DD-15?"

"Yes." Phedra nodded. "She was taking it . . . passing it around to the others. The two of them—they're both guilty!"

"You lie!" snapped Logan.

"No use bluffing," said the tall officer. "We not only have the disc we took from you—but we ran a chemlab test on Jessica's hands. Traces of DD-15 under the nails, in the skin pores. No doubt of it."

Logan tried to stand, but the chair held him. His face was pale with anger. "That's not true! Your test is wrong!"

Was Bracker himself in on this? Logan wondered. Was *he* lying, too? Logan looked at Jessica, but she wouldn't meet his eyes; she stared ahead in shock.

Bracker swung toward the wall, spoke to the voice-cylinder glowing there: "This case is conclusive. We found a disc on Logan 3, and we have lab confirmation on the woman. Plus eyewitness testimony. Verdict?"

A moment of tense silence.

Then the voice-cylinder said calmly: "Execute them."

THE KILLING GROUND

Once, long ago, the country surrounding and encompassing East Africa's great Serengeti Plain swarmed with life. Here, in lazy heat, lion and leopard prowled; the hooves of roan antelope and reedbuck trail-marked the rolling grassland; massive elephants trumpeted the sky, through which the gold-breasted starling and hawk eagle flew; kudu and zebra and gazelle galloped with wildebeest and giraffe; hippos ruled the rivers, while buffalo and bush pig shared the wide savannas; here, too, flourished the horned rhino, the swift impala, the hyena and wild dog. . . .

But now, in this time of Sandman and runner, it was no longer the heartland of life.

The Serengeti was sterile. The great herds were gone; the rivers ran to thin trickles under the high African sun; the brute roar of the king lion was stilled forever.

It was a place of death.

Logan was not prepared for the sentence levied upon him by the computer—that he and Jessica be transported to the Serengeti and left there, on the wide, raw plain, to be hunted by Masai tribesmen and executed by them under official citystate statutes.

On his Earth, condemned criminals were sent to Hell—that vast, deadly ice-shelf stretching between Baffin Bay and the Bering Sea—but here the killing ground was the Serengeti, an area equally as severe and from which escape was equally impossible.

A sealed mazecar whisked them under the Indian Ocean to Mombasa. There they were put into a second car, which arrowed west, into Tanzania—to the platform at Ngorongoro. Another vehicle transfer, and they were flown north to be deposited, for death, on the hot yellow sprawl of the Serengeti.

As they watched, the police paravane lifted free of the plain, angled south, whirred to a tiny glinting dot in the cloudless bowl of sky, then vanished completely.

Leaving them alone.

They had been given a meager ration of water, just enough to keep them alive until the hunters picked up their trail. They wore the basic garb of the condemned: heavy shoes, thin cotton trousers, a sleeved bodyshirt, and a long-billed cap to help fend off the murderous sun. The latter was a necessity, since many bare-headed prisoners had died of sunstroke in earlier days, cheating the Masai of their kill.

There were no lions left to slay. Thus, the pride of a Masai depended on how swiftly and efficiently he could hunt down and execute a condemned man or woman.

Logan and Jessica were, of course, weaponless.

"What do they kill with?" asked Logan.

"Spears," said Jessica. "Tribal tradition. No honor for them in anything else."

"On foot?"

"No, they ride some kind of animal."

"Couldn't," said Logan. "No animals left here." He kicked idly at a bleached buffalo bone half-buried in scrub grass.

"What difference does it make?" asked Jessica tensely. "They're coming for us. That's the only fact that matters."

Logan narrowed his eyes, peering through the heat haze toward a pale blue range of mountainous hills riding the plain's edge.

"If we can make it to those hills, we'll have a better chance . . . get into the rocks and high grass."

"Chance?" She smiled wanly. "We've *no* chance, Logan. No matter where we go they'll find us and they'll kill us. That's their job and they're very good at it."

"Well, our job is to stay alive," said Logan. "So let's get moving."

Before sentence had been passed, Logan had attempted to reach Francis, but no outside contacts were allowed prime citystate violators. He had been stripped of his DS rating and, with it, his potential admission to Godbirth. Which meant he had failed totally in his mission. Once his time had run out here, the aliens would abandon him—whether he lived or died on the Serengeti.

Logan refused to think about this. He had locked his mind on a single goal: survival. Somehow, he would outwit the hunters who stalked him. He and Jessica would survive.

With canteens slung over their shoulders, they set

out across the softly rolling grassland toward the range of northern hills.

The African sun was fierce, an unwinking yellow-white eye of fire, brimming the noon sky, heat-blasting the land. To Logan and Jessica, laboring toward the dim blue hills, it was as if the door of an immense sky-furnace had been opened upon them.

Within a single mile their clothing was sweat-soaked, their ears ringing from the heat.

Logan stopped to look back, shading his eyes.

Jessica stood, head down, gasping from the fiery assault.

"They're coming," said Logan softly.

She blinked tears of salt from her eyes. "How many?"

"I make it . . . three."

Jess nodded. "They usually hunt in a trio."

"And you were right," said Logan. "They *are* mounted. Horses, I think. Probably flown in for them."

Logan estimated the distance left to the edge of the plain. "Cuts our time down, them having horses," he said. "We'll have to run. That's the only way we'll make it."

"In this heat?" She stared at him. "Under this sun?"

He took a quick swallow from his canteen and capped it again. She followed his example. "It's the only sun we've got," he said.

"I can't see how you expect to—"

"Don't talk. Waste of energy."

And he broke into a jogging trot, Jessica beside him.

On and on . . . across the great plain, moving around the heaped bones of elephant and oryx, using ancient trails trod by beasts a century dead, over patches of sandy loam, past solitary clumps of wind-shaped trees. . . .

On and on.

The hills deepened in color. Closer. But the hunters were closer too—close enough now for Jessica to identify the creatures they rode.

"Marabunta!" she said, standing loosely, looking back, dragging furnaced air into her lungs.

Logan had also stopped. Now he twisted toward her, questioning the word.

"Warrior ants," she said. "That's what they're called by the Masai."

He squinted at them in disbelief. "But they— they're the size of *horses!*"

"Could be a mutation," said Jess. "Insects can survive when animals can't."

"Keep going," Logan told her. "We can make it. We're almost there."

They continued to run, throats hot, tongues swollen, their eyes stinging with salt—faint with heat exhaustion. And Logan thought, This is how it was for Doyle, in the desert. Hunters behind with death in their hands and no future ahead, the sun raw on his back, pain racking his legs. . . .

And then, in a final miraculous surge, they were into the blue hills.

Shade. Coolness. Relief.

But no time to rest.

Now a boulder-filled streambed, carpeted in dry white pebbles, with interlacing brush and trees so thickly massed that a tunnel of green formed around them; the smell of wild growth was overpowering, in direct contrast to the arid, burned-ash smell of the plain.

Into high papyrus grass, flowing up five feet above their heads, past yellow-blossomed thorn, around giant trees whose vein-tangled roots snagged at their shoes.

Now into a steep-plunging ravine, grasping at vines to slow their descent, stumbling, sliding downward along a sandy ridge.

At the bottom, in the thick dry silt, under the shade of wide high-trunked trees, they fell to their knees, fighting for breath, holding on to each other like lost children.

"Something . . . to . . ." Logan found it almost impossible to form words; his lips were split and bleeding, ". . . use."

"To use?" Jessica looked at him in confusion.

"Against them . . . to . . . fight them."

She watched him uproot one of the heavy, long-stalked reeds that grew in profusion along the side of the ravine. From his bodyshirt Logan withdrew a jagged-edged bone fragment which he'd found on one of the ancient animal trails. Using strips of vine, he lashed this sharp bone to the end of the reed.

"Spear!" He waved it in triumph.

A sudden spill of gravel and loose stones from the upper ledge of the ravine.

The hunters!

Logan put a hand on Jessica's shoulder, drawing her silently back into the blue-black shadow of the reeds.

Where they waited.

If I can get one of them with this, Logan told himself, gripping his crude weapon, then I can use his spear on the others. I can handle three of them.

But even if you're successful, an inner voice told him, more will come. They'll keep coming, by threes, until they kill you. No way to win. If Doyle had killed both of us back on the desert, more Sandmen would have come. The system works for the hunters, not the hunted.

No way to win.

They had circled, come in from the far side, picking their way carefully along the powdery-dry bed of the ravine, knowing that their quarry was hiding here, run to ground and exhausted, while they were fresh and full of the hunt.

They scanned every thrust of rock, every ridge, every ledge and tree shadow, spears firm in their burnished hands. It was good to hunt again, good to ride the swift marabunta after the condemned ones, good to trail and trap and kill.

Their leader was Duma, named for the cheetah. Tall and slim-bodied, as were all his people, he sat tree-straight in the ant's high saddle, hair swinging behind his shoulders in a roped braid. Raised tribal scars marked his chest and forehead. Duma had been on many hunts, and his skill with a spear was unmatched. Never had Duma missed a living target.

He was the son of their chief, Nyoka, and proud father of the boy who rode beside him this day: eight-year-old Swala, a handsome youth, lithe and quick—and aptly named for the gazelle. This was Swala's first hunt, and his father knew he would do well.

With them rode Nyati—the buffalo—a wise tracker who knew every vine and thorn bush, every ridge and rock and rolling green hill within the Serengeti.

Two masters—and a brave boy who hoped, this day, to become a man.

Duma smiled. The first kill I will take for myself, as elder, for this is custom on a hunt—but the second kill shall be reserved for my son. It shall be Swala's. This had been agreed to by Nyati. The veteran tracker would hold back. For Nyati, there would be other days, other kills, as there had been before—as many as the faces of the night moon.

Beneath Duma, the marabunta paused to swing its giant clicking antennae toward a patch of reed-shadow near the inner ravine wall. The sharp clicking alerted the others.

All were stopped, eyes probing the bank.

"*There*, Father!" shouted young Swala, pointing at Jessica. "A condemned one! Behind the rock."

She stood up, poised to run, inviting the spear of Duma.

He drew back his muscled arm, spearhead glinting in the leaf-filtered sunlight banding the ravine floor. But he did not loose the weapon.

A snake-hiss of sound, and a bone-tipped reed buried itself deep in the warrior's scarred chest just above the heartline. Silently, he toppled from the saddle.

"Father! My father!" cried Swala. He was confused and frightened; his mount swayed back nervously as he fought to control it.

Logan ignored the boy. He charged straight at the second hunter, yanking Nyati's leg violently, pulling

him from the ant's saddle and knocking the spear from
his hand.

An upper-neck chop slammed the Masai, stunned,
into the silt. Logan scooped up the fallen spear,
preparing to drive it into the man's bronzed back,
when he heard Jess scream, "Marabunta!"

Duma's warrior ant was in full attack. The giant
insect reared up, its shining, razored antennae slashing
air, its red and black body towering directly over Logan.

He spun sideways, but his upper shoulder was
opened to the bone by one of the whipping antennae.
The ant moved in, sensing its advantage, jaws wide,
ready to finish the kill. Again Logan pivoted, and,
using his good arm, plunged Nyati's spear into the
creature's bulbous right eye.

Incredibly, smoke and sparks poured from the
wound as the creature went berserk, wildly thrashing
its immense, segmented body to left and right.

A robot, marveled Logan, the thing's a robot!

Now the frenzied ant's left antenna swung up to
knock young Swala from the saddle; the boy fell heavily to the floor of the ravine, striking his head on a
silt-covered rock. He did not move as the maddened
machine-creature reared up to crush him.

Logan sprang between them, driving the boy's
spear full-strength into the ant's vulnerable under-
chest. The great dark insect spun crazily to smash
head-on into the ravine wall, exploding as it hit,
showering the area with bits of broken metal. Then it
lay unmoving, silent, its clockwork interior gutted.

Logan knelt by the unconscious young Masai. Jess
was already there, cradling the boy's bleeding head.

"He's all right," she told Logan.

Nyati had seen it all, seen what this brave white
condemned one had done. He had saved Swala's life.
He had slain the marabunta.

Nyati had seen, and he would remember.

He would never forget.

THE OTHER ME

The trip across the hot plain to the Masai village
was painful for Logan. His shoulder throbbed under the
still-powerful afternoon sun, and the makeshift sling-
bandage was stiff with blood. Jessica had cleaned the
wound with water from the canteens, but there was
very little to be done by way of remedy until they
reached the village.

Jessica rode one of the massive warrior ants with
Swala, who was subdued and aloof, while Logan followed on the second machine-creature. Nyati ran
lightly and easily beside him, sleek-muscled legs piston-
ing over the grass. The Masai was in awe of Logan and
considered it an honor that the white one had chosen
his mount.

A mile short of the village they were met by a
horde of swift-running Masai children who circled Logan and Jessica with saucered eyes. Most of the children had never seen a condemned one alive, and
certainly not astride a marabunta! Ah, what a won-
drous sight this was!

By now the sun had lost most of its force. Afternoon was slowly shading into African night as they dismounted before the hut of the chief.

Nyati, who spoke both English and Swahili, would
be their translator. He would tell the chief of Logan's
deeds.

"You are to wait here," said Nyati.

And he entered the hut, pushing the reluctant
Swala ahead of him. The boy did not relish facing his
grandfather; in *his* eyes he had behaved like a child,

and his grandfather would surely berate him. His father lay dead in a ravine and Swala was not yet a man. It was a day to curse forever!

Outside, the children still circled, gazing wordlessly at the white ones. The adult members of the tribe, in tall brown clusters, kept to a distance, equally curious but uncertain, awaiting the word of their chief. His wisdom would direct them.

"What happens now?" asked Jessica.

"We wait," said Logan. "We stay alive if the chief figures he owes me for saving his grandchild—but we die if he figures me a murderer for killing his son. It could go either way."

She frowned. "Your shoulder's bleeding again."

"I'll be all right," said Logan.

They stood there awkwardly for several long minutes, their fate undecided. Logan ignored the throbbing pain in his shoulder, grateful to have reached the village, grateful for this second chance at life.

Then Nyati appeared, glancing behind him, toward the hut.

"He comes." From the tracker's impassive face it was impossible to guess what the chief might be planning.

Nyoka came out to meet them, looking solemn—a reed-thin, handsome man of indeterminate age, though obviously he was not young. (In this world, Logan realized, the Masai lived and died here in the Serengeti, beyond Sleep, in their own private stratum of society.)

Nyati had explained that their chief was named after the snake. "He is very wise, like the serpent of old," the tracker had told them. "He speaks only wisdom. His words are true, always."

As with all Masai tribesmen, the chief wore a narrow brown cloth slung loosely around his waist. As a badge of rank, a necklace of ivory elephant bones hung from his neck. Each bone in the necklace had been carved into the shape of a snake.

Now he placed a hand on Logan's good arm, speaking slowly and with dignity; his large yellow-brown eyes were deep, and they did not waver from Logan's face.

Nyati translated quietly: "I, Nyoka, salute the condemned one. I declare you a brave warrior. My son died honorably under your spear and for this I hold no anger against you."

Logan exchanged a relieved smile with Jess as the chief continued: "You risked your life to save my grandson, and for this Nyoka is truly in your debt. Your shoulder will be tended. You shall spend the night here in my village, and in the morning, when the sun has shortly risen, we will talk."

And, giving Logan no opportunity to reply, he turned away to reenter the hut.

"It is as I told you," Nyati whispered. "He speaks true wisdom."

Logan nodded. "Indeed he does."

He looked at the red sun through the screening trees as it slid smokily down the horizon. The day was done.

And he was alive.

The Masai were not altogether primitive. Not only did they ride sophisticated robot machines, but their tribal doctor utilized the latest medical knowledge and equipment to maintain group health in the colony.

To their doctor, Logan's shoulder wound was simple, easily treated. By morning it was totally healed. Nothing more than a faint scartrace remained.

Nyoka, true to his word, was ready to talk with Logan shortly after sunup. They met, with Nyati translating, inside the chief's hut, while Jessica waited. ("To him, I don't exist!" she'd complained that morning. And Logan had said, "Wrong. He knows you tried to aid Swala. It's just that his tribal pride dictates that he talk to me, the brave male warrior. But you wouldn't be alive right now if Nyoka didn't appreciate what you did for his grandson.")

A woven reed mat covered the floor of Nyoka's hut. A gold-tipped ceremonial spear was mounted on the wall above the doorway, and a coiled snake, in ebony, formed the centerpiece on a low table of darkly polished wood. Also, among the hut's sparse furnishings: cooking pots and painted hangings, including a lion's head rendered in vivid earth dyes by Nyoka's dead son.

The three men sat down at the low table, and Nyoka spoke first, saying (in translation): "Your wound is healed. You have been fed and you are well rested. It is time for you and the woman to leave our village."

"But we're condemned prisoners." Logan replied, through Nyati. "Where can we go? Even if you allow us to live, even if your warriors no longer ride against us, we are trapped here on the Serengeti."

Slowly, his large eyes intense on Logan, the chief shook his head. "This need not be so. There *is* a way out. But you must go where I direct."

Logan was astonished. "A way *out?* . . . of Serengeti?"

"Perhaps—out of Africa!" And Nyoka smiled for the first time since they'd met; his teeth were even and perfect in wide, pinkish gums.

"Tell me the way!"

The chief spoke in a soft, rhythmic flow, his tone hushed and reverential. Nyati translated as a priest might translate from the Bible.

"You must journey east, to the high mountain of Kilimanjaro. A marabunta will take you. It is nearly a full day's ride. There, upon the insect's back, you will ascend the great mountain. To a ledge high above the plain. Here, at this place, dwells a white leopard, whose eye sees all. The leopard's eye will guide you."

"But how . . . and to where? Guide us where?"

"Seek your answer in the leopard's eye." With this, the chief stood up and put out his hand. "I wish you long life, white one!"

Logan clasped the chief's strong-fingered hand. He was about to speak again, but Nyati shook his head, nodding toward the doorway.

The talk was over.

Logan and Jessica left within the hour, in fresh clothing, with food and water strapped to the ant's saddle, waving farewell to Nyati and to the happy, squealing children who trailed behind them.

Nyoka was not there to see them off—but Swala stood alone beyond the village, at the far edge of the road leading onto the broad plain, watching them until they were out of his range of vision, lost to sight in the wide sea of rolling grass. Then, his face drawn with emotion, head down, he walked back into the village—hating them as he had hated no one else in the whole of his young life.

For Logan and Jess, the ride to Kilimanjaro was one of revelation. They had been through much together, and Jessica felt guilt; she told herself that Logan should know the truth about her, about all this.

She began by saying, "I'm sorry."

"For what?"

"For the fact that you're here . . . that you're going through all this because of me."

"We're going through it *together*," said Logan. "And because of Phedra, not you."

They rode in silence for several moments, Jessica directly behind him in the ant's saddle. She hesitated, forming the proper words; the words were very important.

"I want to tell you everything," she said. "I want you to have the truth."

Logan turned his head to smile at her. "It's a long ride. My belly's full. My shoulder's healed. My head is shaded. My thirst is satisfied. . . ." Patting the canteen at his side. "So, if you want to talk, I've got nothing to do but listen."

"I'm serious, Logan. I'm not joking."

"Go on," he said.

"The day you came to my unit . . . to tell me about Doyle," she began, her voice steady and resigned, "I was pretending. I *pretended* to be cold to the news of his suicide."

"You had me convinced," said Logan.

"The hard way I talked . . . the drinks . . . the part about Doyle being a fool. It was all an act. Actually, I was dying inside."

"But why the act?"

"I'll get to that. At the time, all that mattered was

that I threw you off balance . . . I wanted to appear cool and sensual . . . make you desire me."

"Well, it worked."

"Exactly as I'd planned. Entice you to that party in Arcade, excite you, then have sex with you back at my unit—so I could plant the DD-15 in your jacket."

Logan twisted in the saddle to face her. "*You* planted the Dust on me?"

"I hated you. I blamed you for hounding my brother to suicide. I loved Doyle deeply . . . deeply . . . and I blamed you for his death."

Just as *she* did, thought Logan, in *my* world.

"I wanted to avenge him, pay you back for what you'd done to him, to me . . . and planting that Dust on you seemed the best way."

"But Phedra was at Headquarters," protested Logan. "*She* was the one who accused both of us."

Jessica nodded. "She simply used an opportunity she never thought she'd get. You were right, she *was* jealous when she saw us together in Arcade—and she must have found the drug disc in my things when I was at the gallery."

"You took the disc there?"

"Yes—to try to slip it into your jacket if my full plan didn't work out, in case I couldn't lure you back to my unit. Phedra saw her chance, and framed the whole story of us using the drug together."

"And she had *no* idea you intended planting it on me?"

"No idea at all." She smiled thinly. "But it certainly helped verify her story."

"But why tell me all this now?" asked Logan. "You didn't have to."

She sighed, spilling out the words: "What you did for the boy, for Swala . . . I couldn't hate you after that. You can't help being what you are . . . the system gets us all eventually. It got you—and it got Doyle. All my life I've hated the system. It killed Doyle, and now it's killing us."

Logan was hard-struck by her words. She was telling him the truth, he knew; it *had* been an act, her coldness, her lack of compassion—the things that had shocked and revolted him about her.

She *was* like Jessica after all! They were as mentally alike as they were physically alike! And since she had told him the truth about herself, he owed her the same kind of honesty, if only to erase the image of the uniformed DS killer in her mind.

"Turns out we were *both* putting on acts," he declared.

"What do you mean?"

"I'm not the man you think I am. I'm not Logan 3."

Her eyes widened. "But you are! I've seen you on the tri-dims. I recognized you instantly when you came to my unit."

"I look like him—exactly like him—and his name is mine, but I'm no killer, Jess! I hate this system as much as you do, so much that I once helped destroy one just like it on my world. . . ."

And, as they rode, as the scorched brown land passed beneath them under the steady march of the marabunta and the sun fell slowly down the western sky, Logan told her everything. About the aliens, the dual worlds, his mission here . . . and about his own wife and child, his own Jessica.

When he finished, she was crying softly, her head pressed forward against his shoulder, her arms tight around his waist.

"I tried to *kill* you," she sobbed. "I did this to you. How will you ever get back to her now? To the other me . . . to your son."

"I'll do what Nyoka told me to do," said Logan quietly. "He's a wise man, Jess. He knows this land. There may really be a way out."

He kissed her cheek, gently.

Ahead of them, blue and steep-rising and mysterious, at the far edge of the vast plain, the mountain waited.

THE LEOPARD'S EYE

And, at last, they were here.

Kilimanjaro.

The king of peaks—rising in snowcapped majesty more than nineteen thousand feet into the African sky, a blue-white mammoth to stun the mind, a thing of myth and mystery . . .

At the lower slope, looking up, Logan and Jessica felt the power and immensity of the mountain, a palpable presence around them. They could not imagine scaling this massive stone citadel. Where was the ledge? How could they possibly reach it?

"There's no way up for us," said Jessica.

"Nyoka told me, 'Upon the insect's back you will ascend the great mountain.' We'll have to trust our robot friend here to do the job," said Logan.

"You mean, the ant *knows* where to go?"

"He was programmed to get us this far. I figure he's also programmed to find the ledge. Just hang tight."

And Logan nudged the marabunta forward.

Obeying preset tapes, the giant metal insect began ascending the slope, moving with surety over ancient trails and along narrow rock fissures, climbing steadily higher on its six legs, transporting its fragile human cargo slowly upward on this final stage of their journey.

The heat of the plains had now given way to the blowing cold of the upper mountain, and Logan halted the marabunta long enough for them to put on the

64

thermosuits and snowgoggles Nyoka had provided. The light duraloid suits, strong and flexible, had built-in heat controls that adjusted automatically to maintain normal body temperature.

"At least we won't freeze," said Logan, tabbing up his suit.

"What about the leopard?" asked Jess. "If there really is one up here, won't we need some kind of weapon to defend ourselves?"

"If a weapon was needed, Nyoka would have provided one," said Logan. "The leopard's obviously no threat. Whatever it is, it can't be alive."

"A robot," said Jess. "It could be a machine—like this ant."

"Maybe. But we won't know till we get there."

Now the lumbering insect moved upward on a path that laboriously followed the contour of the mountain's flank. This path had been carved from the iced rock centuries ago, had taken many years to complete, at a staggering cost in human life, and was a marvel of engineering. At no time, despite the foul weather and the incredible height they'd attained, did Logan feel threatened or uneasy. The way was safe.

As a young man, had Nyoka trod this same path?

Their climb ended at a high shelf of wind-packed snow. Here the marabunta stopped, became motionless.

"This must be the ledge," said Logan.

He and Jess dismounted, heads lowered against the gusting ice wind. In touching ground, Logan's left foot dislodged a rock, which dropped from the ledge, booming down the rugged flank of the mountain.

Jessica spoke against Logan's ear in the moaning wind: "There's nothing here. Not *anything*."

Logan moved closer to the mountain, peering through his goggles. He pointed. "Cave!"

Logan guided Jess past a curtain of blowing white as the shelf area deepened into blackness.

Inside, the wind decreased sharply. Normal conversation was possible.

As his eyes adjusted to the gloom, Logan examined one of the cave walls. It was smooth.

"This is man-made," he said, running his fingers along the marbled surface. "Like the path—somebody carved it."

"But why? For what purpose?"

"Probably built as a shrine . . . long ago," said Logan. "For tribal worship."

Jessica pointed ahead. "There's some kind of light!"

Deep in the man-carved cave, a pale green radiance tinted the curving walls.

They started toward it.

Suddenly Logan tensed, put his hand on Jessica's arm. "Listen!"

A rumble. Faint, and high above them, but increasing by the second. It grew to a roar, a tumbling cataract of sound.

"What *is* it?"

"Avalanche!" shouted Logan, sprinting for the outer ledge.

It must have been the small stone he dislodged. All it takes up here, he thought; the concussion from a single dropped stone can set things moving.

Get to the ant! Get him into the cave before—

Too late!

The metal creature was already going, caught in the downpouring rush of rock and snow, swept from the ledge like a giant toy, instantly lost in the white flood.

Jessica caught up with Logan, clutching his arm, watching the great mountain shake its skin.

The rumble was now a constant skull-stabbing roar that drove them back from the ledge. They were being sealed in; the sky in front of them was quickly being extinguished as the bouldered mass filled the cave's entrance, cutting off the late-day sun and placing them, finally, in total darkness.

It ended.

The last shiverings of rock spatted against the ledge; the snowdust settled. Full cycle: rumble to roar to snow-velvet silence. Again, the mountain slept.

"One thing's for sure," said Logan. "We won't be going back down."

They turned toward the faint illumination at the cave's end, walking slowly, allowing the furor to ease inside them. Kilimanjaro had shown its might, and they were stunned and shaken by the display.

"Are you frightened?" asked Logan.

"No," said Jess. "Maybe I should be—but somehow I believe what Nyoka told you. About the leopard's eye. It will show us a way out of the mountain."

"If there *is* a leopard," said Logan.

"We wouldn't be here unless he knew," said Jessica. "He programmed the ant to take us here."

"And the ant's gone," said Logan. "Maybe we were meant to ride it back down to the plain. Nyoka didn't count on an avalanche."

They reached the source of illumination, rounded a bend in the cave, looked up.

The leopard was above them, on a carved shelf of rock, poised to leap, frozen there in a timeless moment of attack, the ridged muscles along his sleek flank etched in perfect simulation, tail caught in mid-lash, ears twitched back, flattened into the graceful head. A ton of white ivory shaped to the likeness of a crouching beast. In the exact center of its lowered head, a matchless, square-cut green-glowing emerald eye, the size of a man's fist.

"He's beautiful," said Jess in a hushed tone. "I've never seen anything so beautiful . . . so *alive!*"

"Well, if he's alive he's not telling us anything," said Logan.

"Perhaps he will," said Jess. "This is a shrine, Logan. How about some faith?"

"I don't believe in building shrines to anything—not even white leopards. And the only faith I have is in *me.*"

"Spoken like a true Sandman."

"I was one. I'm not anymore."

"Well, you *sound* like one. Arrogant, and so sure of your rightness!"

"This kind of talk won't get us out of here," said Logan. "I'm climbing up to have a go at that eye."

He scrambled up to the rock shelf, reached the

head of the carved beast, and began prodding and pulling at the emerald.

"Is it loose?" asked Jess. "Does it move?"

Logan shook his head. He stepped back, consider-
ing alternatives. "If I had a knife I could pry it loose.
Should have brought along one of Nyoka's spears."

"You think there's something behind it . . . a
map, directions of some kind?"

"That's what I'm thinking." Logan nodded. He
picked up a sharp-edged rock fragment and began digging at the large green emerald. After several minutes
he pulled back, sighing. "No good. Can't even scratch
it."

The green stone was not meant to be removed, so
his guess had been wrong. He was deeply discouraged.
A sense of panic was edging into his mind. What good
would a map do them, even if they found one, trapped
here inside the damned mountain? The ant was gone
and, with it, all their food and water. The cave entrance was completely blocked, so there was no way to
reach the path leading down. And even if they got
down onto the plain again, how long could they last?

To Logan, at this moment, Nyoka's words of escape were hollow and meaningless. What if the clever
Masai had never really intended for them to escape?
What if sending them here to this empty shrine to die
was his way of avenging the son Logan had slain on
the Serengeti? The avalanche had simply aided and
abetted the process. A bonus for old Nyoka.

Jessica's excited voice broke into his dark
thoughts. She was calling him.

"Logan, down here!"

He slid quickly from the shelf to join her where
she knelt at the opposite wall of the cave.

"What have you found?"

"Nothing . . . yet," she told him. "But I think I
know what Nyoka meant when he said, 'The leopard's
eye will guide you.' "

"Well?" he urged.

"If you sight along the trajectory—the line of his
sight, given his position on the ledge—you arrive here.
He's looking at *this* section of wall."

They were both running their hands over the smooth stone. It seemed to hold no secrets.

"Here," said Jess. "I've found something!"

At cave-floor level, a small metal knob ran flush with the wall, almost invisible in the glowing green darkness. Jess poked at it, tried to twist it, but the knob did not move.

Logan studied it. "I'd say it's a control lever," he declared. "Could be operated by foot pressure. Let's find out."

And he stood, placing his right shoe over the knob and pressing his weight against it.

The knob moved!

And, in a steady, grinding motion, the section of wall slid back to reveal a descending flight of crude-cut stone steps. Muted daylight from a distant rock fissure barely illuminated the passageway as they hurried downward.

At the bottom, the passage opened abruptly into a rust-red, alum-braced tunnel, dead-ending at the steps. Logan ran a finger along the dirt-grimed curve of metal.

"Mazeway!" he said. "A spur track through the mountain. Never completed."

Jessica's excitement dimmed as she examined the tunnel floor. "But there's no grid," she told Logan. "A mazecar can't run without one."

"Not here, on the spur," he said. "But if we follow this tunnel far enough . . ."

"Then Nyoka was telling you the truth," said Jessica, her face bright again. "A way out of Serengeti—out of Africa!"

They looked at each other, exchanging foolish, dazed smiles.

The trek down the tunnel was silent. They knew they were not free, and their initial exuberance had given way to darker introspection. Once they managed to locate a mazecar, they had no safe destination to seek. They were condemned fugitives and would be executed on sight if they attempted to return to Angeles

Complex. And without valid citystate ID, no Complex anywhere on Earth was safe for them.

"Where do we go, Logan?"

He walked the gloomed tunnel in silent thought. Then he stopped, turned to her. "We've got one possible chance."

"Yes?"

"There's a man the aliens told me about—a man they said I could contact in case of emergency. Named Kirov. Works for Central Control in Moscow. If we can reach him there before we're caught, he just might have an answer for us, a way for us to survive."

"Survive," said Jessica softly. She smiled. "Right now, that's the most beautiful word on Earth!"

The spur tunnel ended two miles beyond Kilimanjaro, at an abandoned maze-intersect grid.

"Are you sure we can get a car?" asked Jessica as they mounted the brush-covered platform.

Logan moved to a rusted callbox, pulling creeper roots and vines free of its face. "If this box is still connected to the main grid, I can rig it for a car," he said.

He finished clearing the box, prying loose a side control plate, reaching inside to examine the wiring pattern. An orange spark sizzled against his hand, and Logan grinned. He carefully reconnected two multicolored wire clusters, using his metal beltclasp as a makeshift tool.

Within seconds, in a humming rush, a mazecar slotted into the platform.

"This is an unauthorized area," the car told them as they stripped their thermosuits and climbed inside. "It is not permitted to transport citizens in this area without central clearance. Please identify for clearance."

And the car waited, unmoving, on the grid.

Logan leaned forward, and smashed the machine's auto-destination device. The car-voice sputtered: "Not . . . is . . . citizens . . . this . . . proceed . . . not for . . ."

The voice rattled and died.

"You killed it!" exclaimed Jess. "Now we can't move!"

"I'll take us in on manual," he told her, activating the emergency control panel inside the car.

"Won't they stop us?"

"They won't know. This will go on the board at CenComp as a routine vehicle malfunction. By the time they've triangulated the problem and sent a repair team we'll be in Moscow."

"You've done this kind of thing before, haven't you?"

"In my world I was a runner, Jess—just like your brother."

She looked at him, her eyes probing his face. "There's so much more I'd like to know about you," she said as the car left the platform and began skimming along the grid.

"You know too much already," said Logan. "The aliens warned me not to contact you. If I'd listened to them, you wouldn't be here now, involved in all this. It's not your problem."

"The system *is* my problem," she said levelly. "And maybe the aliens were right. . . . Knowing you has given me hope. Maybe you *can* destroy this system."

"Right now I'm a long way from doing it," he said.

The silver mazecar, at full acceleration, jetted them through the gleaming tunnel under the African night.

Away from Kilimanjaro. Away from the Serengeti.

They had escaped the killing ground.

A SANDMAN'S GUN

Kirov 2 was a small, pale man of bland personality and rigid habit. The bed in his modest lifeunit (in the village of Leninskiye, thirty-five kilometers from central Moscow) faced east. At dawn each morning, as the sun's fingers touched Kirov's thin eyelids, he would wake instantly, cleanse himself, put on his freshly-pressed state uniform, dial a frugal breakfast from the vending slots (the fried-eggs-on-wheat-no-butter-with-orange-juice menu never varied), and take a local mazecar into Moscow.

Emerging on the busy platform beneath Red Square, he would take a riser up, walk briskly across the wide cobbled Square, past Lenin's red-granite tomb alongside the high Kremlin wall, to enter the Kremlin itself through the gate of Spasskaya Tower.

As a Class A computer tech in the Georgievsky Hall of the Great Kremlin Palace, Kirov was always the first to arrive for work each day. He would solemnly begin his duties at a CenControl data feedback unit board under one of the six huge bronze chandeliers (no longer operational) lining the vast, gold-painted ceiling.

Kirov 2 was neither liked nor disliked by his fellow workers; they ignored him completely as he ignored them. He performed his job with quiet efficiency. If asked a question, he would answer it in a calm, evenly controlled tone of voice. Otherwise, he said nothing.

His future was in perfect order. On red, Kirov had already chosen a Sleepshop in Revolution Square, off the Bolshoi Arcade, which he would enter on his twenty-first birthday. Deep Sleep, for him, would be calmly accepted as part of his duty to the system that supported him. He would make his personal contribution to global birth control without fear or regret.

Kirov had no memory whatever of being taken, one night, aboard a great silver ship—nor of the mental indoctrination he had received there. All knowledge of this encounter with the aliens had been erased from his conscious mind.

Thus, Kirov 2, who considered himself a very ordinary citizen, was actually very special: he was Logan's only contact between two worlds.

The gridline from Kilimanjaro to Moscow took them directly north, through Kenya and Ethiopia, under the Red Sea and beneath the tip of Saudi Arabia, on beneath Syria and Turkey and the Black Sea, into Russia. And, finally, under the Moskva River, to Red Square.

Logan slotted the mazecar into a side repair-platform and quickly exited with Jess. They took an expressbelt up to the Square.

He'd been given no instructions on how to contact Kirov, but Logan knew that the man worked inside the Kremlin, once the seat of Soviet government and now headquarters for CenControl. Upon questioning a guard there, he learned that Kirov was on dayshift and would leave, with the other day workers, through Spasskaya Gate within the hour.

The weather was mild and clear; a soft breeze from the Moskva carried the sharp scent of fir trees into the Square as Logan waited with Jess in the shadow of St. Basil's, under the huge fire-colored onion domes.

He had asked the guard for a description of Kirov and had been told not to worry. "Can't miss him," the guard had declared. "Always the last out. Every day the same, you can depend on it. First in, last out. No way to miss Kirov."

*   *   *

It had been an uneventful day, as were all days to Kirov 2. Upon completing his stint at the board, he had left with his fellow workers, but, as was his custom, he had returned after punchout to examine the historical tapestry, threaded in gold, which ran the entire 200-foot length of the hall. Kirov did this each day after boardtime, carefully savoring a small segment of the tapestry during each visit. It took him exactly two months of working days to progress from the first section of this masterwork to its end. And after completing this inspection he would begin the next afternoon to slowly repeat the process. It was one of the few pleasant activities Kirov enjoyed in his dull, self-limited existence.

As predicted, he was last through the gate under the long-silent clock chimes of the Spasskaya Tower. Looking neither right nor left, he walked briskly across the Square to the maze entry.

Logan and Jess followed.

At the platform, Kirov settled into the rear of a local mazecar. As the car moved out along the tunnel, Kirov was startled to feel a hand at his shoulder.

"Kirov 2?"

He blinked. "I am that person."

"I'm Logan 3. I've come to you for help."

He started to protest that he had never heard the name, and could not be of help to strangers, when something deep in his mind responded. Kirov nodded. "We will talk in my unit," he said quietly.

And they rode in silence to Leninskiye.

Kirov's lifeunit was as colorless and pale as the little man himself. The interior was painted a drab gray; there were no decorations of any kind to brighten the walls; heavy drapes obscured the view, and the furniture was starkly functional. The unit was, however, scrubbed and spotless. Not a mote of dust was allowed to settle there, since Kirov was an obsessively clean man.

Inside, before speaking, he prepared a pot of rather bitter yellow tea for his guests, bade them sit down, and then asked, sipping his sugarless brew, how he might help.

"We need to establish new identities," Logan told him. "As Logan 3 and Jessica 6, we're fugitives. If we're taken by the Federal Police we'll be executed. We need new IDs."

Kirov spoke in a flat monotone: "I don't know why you came to me, or who sent you, and I certainly don't know why I am willing to help you—but I *am* willing to do so." He stroked his thinly bearded chin. "I seem to be *impelled* to help you, which I find most strange. Normally, I would turn both of you over to the authorities."

Logan realized that the aliens had mentally prepared Kirov on a subliminal basis and that the little man knew nothing of his having been influenced by them. Which was all right with Logan, if that's how they wanted it. All that mattered was the help he needed.

"Exactly what do you wish me to do?" Kirov asked.

"Arrange complete new identities for us both. Do you have internal access to the Central Computer?"

"Yes."

"We'll provide you with basic data. You simply program it into the board. Can you do that?"

Kirov nodded. "But you must understand my problem. The board will automatically cancel the new identities—when it becomes obvious, in cross-check, that your crystal patterns do not match."

Jess put aside her tea (having found it undrinkable). "How long can we count on getting by with the new IDs?" she asked.

"Six hours maximum," said Kirov. "Normally, a cross-check would be instantaneous, but I can delay the process for six hours. Will this be sufficient?"

Jess turned to him: "*Will* it, Logan?"

"All we need to do is find Francis. Once we do, he can get our cases reversed and *prove* that Phedra lied. Finding him shouldn't take long. He's our key back into the system."

Kirov stood up, collected the tea things, and took

them into the service cubicle. Logan followed him there.

"When can we expect to have ID clearance?"

"As soon as you have brought me a DS Gun," Kirov said in his flat monotone. "Would you care for a vitaflake biscuit?"

"Wait, I—" Logan started to protest.

"Perhaps *you*," said Kirov, returning to Jessica with a plate of biscuits. She shook her head.

Kirov sat down in a stiff-backed chair, nibbling on one of the biscuits. Logan stood above him, glaring.

"You seem angry," said the little man.

"What's this about my bringing you a Gun?"

"A Sandman's Gun . . . I have . . . a sudden urge to possess this weapon."

"But a citizen can't even *touch* one," said Logan. "Each Gun is coded to its operative. If I tried to steal one for you it would take my arm off!"

"Only *after* the detonation device has been set," said Kirov. "If you took a Gun from the line, at the factory in Monte Carlo, *before* the device has been set—there would be no problem."

"Is he serious about this?" Jess asked Logan.

"Oh, let me assure both of you, I am quite serious," said Kirov, dusting his hands into a naptowel. "I must have the Gun before I can help you."

"But I can't leave Jess!"

"She can remain here in my unit until you return with the weapon." He looked at Jess with his flat, dull eyes. "You shall be quite safe here." He smiled faintly. "I will admit that my request for a Gun is at direct odds with my pacifist personality, but this is nevertheless what I demand if you wish my help."

"The factory is impossible to penetrate," Logan declared. "There's no way I could reach the Gunline."

"Incorrect," said Kirov. "Tomorrow, at my board, I will program you as a Gun Controller, Class A, which will guarantee clear entry into the factory." He shrugged a thin shoulder. "The rest is up to you."

Logan studied the pale little man for a long moment.

"And if you are thinking that perhaps you could

betray me, use your new ID to hunt down your friend—I merely remind you of the woman. I shall turn her over to the police for immediate execution if you do not return here with the weapon directly from Monte Carlo."

"We must do what he wants," Jess told Logan. "There's no other way."

Logan nodded, his eyes hard on Kirov. "You'll have your Gun."

And Kirov smiled again, a soft wet smile. "That will be very nice," he said.

AT MONTE CARLO

A silver needle threading earth, the mazecar blazed south, beneath the Carpathian Mountains, through Hungary—then west, under the tip of Yugoslavia, into Italy, and on below the French coast to the platform at Nice.

Using his new ID, as Prestor 8, Logan rented a hoverstick for the short jump to Monte Carlo. If he ran into trouble at the Gunfactory, using the maze could be risky; the jet-powered Devilstick would provide a much more reliable method of escape from the area.

Coming in by air, riding the stick high above the wide sweep of sun-sparked Mediterranean, Logan was impressed by the idyllic setting: perched on its high white limestone cliff above the sea, Monte Carlo resembled a mythic giant's castle of crystal and glass. Threemile units rose glittering into the clean arc of sky in pinks, soft greens, pastel blues . . . Date palm and Barbary fig trees dotted the high terraces; scarlet Riviera flowers bloomed in lush profusion.

Difficult to think of this romantic area as what it really was: a dispenser of death, origin of nightmare destructive force, the primary world source of DS weaponry.

Logan was still mystified by Kirov's bizarre demand. It might be explained as the manifestation of a latent dominance syndrome, previously blocked and buried in the frustrated little man and activated by the sudden realization that he finally had total power over others, that the lives of Logan and Jessica were truly in his hands. It was obviously something the aliens had not anticipated, a random personality flaw that Logan was now forced to accommodate.

He had seriously considered stealing a Gun, still holstered, from a Sandman. The attack itself would be relatively simple: Logan would strike down the DS man and take the belted Gun before other Sandmen arrived. Simple. But then he would face the supremely difficult task of defusing the weapon.

Once, on his return from Argos, he had actually accomplished this. Unsure of the dangers he'd be facing on Earth, Logan had taken a holstered weapon from the body of a dead Sandman, brought the Gun into camp, and, using special tools, painstakingly defused it, recoding it to his hand-pattern. He had put it away, vowing he would never use it. But when the Borgia Riders took Jess . . .

The situation was different now. Even if he could succeed in using his specialized knowledge of weaponry to defuse a Gun for Kirov, there were no devastated cities in which to obtain the necessary tools. Also, the theft of the Gun would be flashed on every DS alert board; Sandmen would converge on the area, sealing off all escape routes.

No; the only way to satisfy Kirov was to obtain a Gun from the line. A line Gun, not yet keyed in to the boards, would present less direct risk. And if I'm clever enough, Logan told himself, perhaps the weapon will never be missed.

It was possible.

Just barely possible.

Monte Carlo's casino was once its heart—the lure that attracted moneyed gamblers of all nations. Here, under marbled Victorian arches, fortunes had been won and lost on the single oiled spin of a soft-clicking wheel. Counts and grand dukes wagered castle and mistress on the maddening caprice of a tiny, dancing ivory ball. Many ended as suicides, leaping from the high cliff into the depths of the Mediterranean, as the green baize tables and rosewood roulette wheels took their toll.

But the opulent casino was gone; its marbled splendor had given way to the stark gray bulk of a Gunfactory that now dominated Casino Hill. The graceful arches and red-velvet pillars were replaced by metalloid assembly lines and by emotionless robots that regulated the constant flow of weaponry.

From these steel corridors emerged Fuser and Lasercannon, Stunrifle and Pinbeamer—but the major product was the Gun, the deadly homer-carrying DS killweapon that haunted the mind of every runner.

"Prestor 8," Logan had said to the ID roboguard outside the main assembly block. "Control."

"Purpose of visit?"

"Routine line check."

"Identify," said the robot.

Logan stepped inside the scanroom and casually wall-slotted the Gun tech foilcard provided by Kirov. If the ID failed, he would never leave this room alive.

The chamber weighed him, photochecked him, scanned his body profile—computer-matching man to foilcard.

A screen in front of Logan flashed the readout:

> PRESTOR 8—96466
> GUN CONTROL TECHNICIAN
> CLASS A

The screen ran a complex cross-pattern of coded numbers so rapidly that Logan's eye could not follow them.

Then, in green, the word he'd waited for: VERIFIED.

The heavy duralloy slidedoor to the assembly block opened for him.

Verified!

He was inside.

Calmly, slowly, Logan walked toward the Guns.

Installation of the pore-pattern detonation device represented the final stage of Gun assembly. Therefore, Logan deliberately initiated his inspection just short of the area.

Logan was comfortable in his role as a Gun tech; his basic working knowledge of DS weaponry enabled him to pull off the impersonation without strain. He was smooth and professional, and the drone robots ignored him as he performed his duties, picking various weapons from the line, checking them carefully, making rapid notations in the minibook he carried.

As Logan moved down the line, the chief section robot approached him. He stared at Logan with faceted, lidless metal eyes.

"I assume you wish to test-fire one of our products?"

"Uh . . . naturally," said Logan.

"Then select a weapon of your choice," said the robot, "and please follow me."

Logan was annoyed at this delay. He wanted to get the job over quickly, since his unauthorized position here was extremely dangerous. What if they contacted CIC? What if the Central Inspection Control office was asked about Prestor 8? No, we didn't send him. No, he shouldn't be at your factory.

Every minute wasted here placed Logan in deeper jeopardy.

He selected a weapon and followed the tall humanoid robot. He had not planned on firing any of the Guns, but apparently this was part of a normal tech inspection. It was expected. No way of avoiding it.

The test area, to the left of the main assembly floor, contained several targets of varying size, mounted at widely spaced intervals across the width of a sound-and-shock-insulated firing tunnel.

The section robot handed Logan a silver ammopac stamped with the factory's black death-head design.

"Six charges," he said. "Full pac."

Logan armed the Gun, weighing it in his hand.

"You'll note the balance has been improved," said the tall robot. "Barrel-weight reduction, mainly. But with absolutely no loss of basic reliability."

"I can feel the difference," said Logan.

The Gun's long barrel gleamed under the factory lights; its pearl handle was snug against his palm and cool to the touch. Seductive. The damned Gun was always seductive.

"I suggest you try a ripper," said the robot. "You'll find that we have increased its force considerably."

Logan raised the weapon, set to ripper, and sighted the nearest target: a block of solid double-band durasteel.

He triggered the Gun.

The block instantly erupted into a snowfall of tiny steel fragments.

"Improved?" asked the robot.

"Improved." Logan nodded. "Definitely an upgrade of overall destruct power."

The robot seemed pleased. "Care to try a tangler? ... The new stress-webbing is—"

"Thanks, but I've seen enough here," said Logan.

"The tensile strength has been *doubled*. You really should try one."

"I'm on a tight schedule," said Logan, handing him the Gun. "But I'll make special note of it in my report."

The machine trailed Logan back to the Gunline, still talking about basic product improvement.

"We never consider any design totally perfected," he declared. "Most Sandmen don't appreciate that fact. They fail to realize that they have *us* to thank for a higher killscore each year."

How do I get rid of him? Logan knew that with this overzealous robot watching his slightest move, it would be utterly impossible for him to remove a line Gun.

Even more unsettling, if he actually managed to steal a weapon, how would he get it past the scanners? All visitors, including techs, were scanchecked when entering or leaving the factory grounds. You didn't just walk out with a Gun.

Or *did* you?

Suddenly, logically, Logan had the answer.

No scanchecks were made on section robots leaving the factory. That was *why* only machines were employed here: they could be programmed against theft. Exit checks were unnecessary.

Logan smiled at the robot. "You seem to be exceptionally well versed in Gun design."

"It is my specialty," said the tall machine.

"I know this is an unusual request—but I would like to take you back to CIC with me, have you talk to my superiors. I think you'd be able to provide invaluable suggestions in relation to future line-inspection procedure."

"That is most flattering," said the robot. "Of course, since this is your wish, I would be willing to accompany you."

Logan shut the minibook, tucking it inside his green worktunic. "I wish to leave immediately. Will this cause you any problem?"

"None whatever," said the machine.

"Let's meet outside the main gate. I have a hoverstick there."

The robot nodded.

"And, ah . . ." Logan added casually, "you'd better take one of the new line Guns along—to demonstrate what you've been telling me."

"Very well," said the humanoid, slipping a weapon into his sidepouch.

Logan smiled at him once more, then turned for the exit—but the robot's metallic voice stopped him.

"Prestor 8?" The tall machine was staring at him.

What's wrong, Logan wondered? What mistake did I make? Does he know who I am?

"I wish to say, Prestor 8, that I consider this an honor."

"Well . . ." said Logan, drawing in a breath. "You have certainly earned it."

The robot said nothing more, and Logan watched him walk stiffly toward the machine-exit.

Halfway to Nice, along a rocky coastal section of the French Riviera, Logan brought the hoverstick down on the long-abandoned motor-vehicle highway notched into the cliff face.

"Why are we stopping?" asked the robot.

"Just couldn't resist," Logan said, climbing from the control seat. The robot also dismounted. As Logan cut the power, the hoverstick settled to the ancient, sun-cracked asphalt.

"Might I inquire as to precisely what you could not resist?"

"The view," said Logan, looking over the highway's edge at the blue-green Mediterranean far below. The cliff rose sheer at their backs, dropping sharply to the sea in front of them. The roar of water against rock drifted up faintly, reduced to a near-whisper at this high altitude.

Logan shook his head slowly. "Beautiful, isn't it?"

"I'm afraid that the appreciation of natural beauty is a gift I have been denied," said the machine.

"Too bad," Logan sighed. "But at least I think you'll agree that this is an ideal place to try out that Gun of yours."

The robot's lidless eyes studied Logan. "Not permitted," he said.

"But I thought you wanted me to test-fire the tangler?"

"That is true—but not here, not at this location," explained the machine. "A Gun may not be fired under any circumstances outside the factory test area."

"Then at least let me examine it again," said Logan. "I won't attempt to fire it."

"Not permitted," repeated the robot. "Outside the factory, the weapon must never leave my possession. I can demonstrate it to your superiors at CIC under controlled conditions, but I am not permitted, at any time, to hand the weapon over to you."

"I see."

"It is my hope that you will not find my attitude offensive," said the machine. "I am acting under strict rules that do not permit me to fulfill your request."

Logan nodded, mentally weighing his chances against the machine. Not good. He couldn't employ omnite, or any other normally effective physical combat technique—since foot or hand blows, no matter how expertly delivered, would inflict no damage whatever on that tall metal body. And he had no weapon.

Yet, he told himself, I *must* obtain the Gun.

Logan knelt beside the silent Devilstick, fiddling with its control panel. "This thing's been acting strange," he said. "I think the lower needle jet is losing power."

"I observed no such malfunction in flight," said the robot.

"Let me try it alone. Less weight strain on the pod. Maybe I can figure out what's wrong." Logan activated the stick. "I'll just circle a couple of times. . . ."

"As you wish." The robot nodded. "But the device seems quite sound to me."

And he stepped back as Logan roared the stick skyward.

In the air, he estimated the space between the robot and the cliff. Room enough, he decided, if I come in fast and keep the sea at my back.

Logan circled once as the robot peered upward.

Fast and simple, Logan told himself.

And he powered the Devilstick, full-thrust, at the robot, skimming in low over the highway to drive the stick's sharp duralloy nose directly into the creature's metal chest.

The impact smashed the humanoid into the base of the rock with incredible force. Logan powered the stick swiftly upward again, fighting to regain full control. The cliff seemed to leap at him as he swung the craft hard-left to avoid violent collision with the rock face.

Below, the big robot lay motionless, metal parts strewn along the cracked road surface.

Logan brought the hovercraft down directly beside the body, quickly dismounting. He rolled the heavy creature over on its side, unsnapped the robot's carrier-pouch, and pulled the Gun free.

At last! He had it!

"Stop!" said the machine, staggering up to face Logan. "Not . . . permitted."

The creature's chest was a smoking mass of shattered metal and ruptured circuitry. One of its arms had been totally ripped away; loose wires dangled from the gaping shoulder. And, in striking the rocks, the left side of its head had been crushed flat. The robot's one still-functional eye was canted at a grotesque angle.

To Logan, the machine now seemed a totally alien thing, the thin veneer of pseudo-humanity having been ripped away.

The robot advanced on Logan as he retreated toward the road edge.

"Stay back!" And Logan brought up the Gun.

The machine kept coming, its twisted mouth forming the same ominous phrase: "Not permitted . . . not permitted."

But the ammopac had been removed and Logan couldn't fire; the Gun was useless.

Jamming the weapon into his belt, he feinted left, then lunged right, attempting to put the machine between himself and the road edge. And did not succeed.

The creature slammed its arm across Logan's face, spilling him to the highway. Dazed, only half-conscious, he was powerless to resist as the tall machine plucked him up and swung his body toward the edge of the cliff.

"Not permitted . . ." the creature rasped. "Not permitted . . ."

And Logan was hurled from the cliff—a sheer mile drop to the distant sea.

As he went over, the instinct to survive fired his blood, and Logan clawed wildly at an overhang of heavy brush growing along a narrow ledge of rock, obtained a handhold—and managed to check his fall.

Loosened at its base, the tough-rooted brush

threatened to pull free of the rock, but held. For how long?

Logan hung there, swinging by one hand, as the robot's twisted metal head loomed above him. Can the damn thing reach me? No, Logan assured himself. Can't. I'm too far down.

The creature realized that in order to dislodge this man below him, in order to send him plunging into the sea, it would be necessary to climb down to him. He set out to do this, easing his battered metal body over the road edge. . . .

Logan, hanging ten feet below, no longer thought about his enemy; he was now trying desperately to obtain a double-handed grip on the slipping brush. But each time he hauled himself a bit higher, the shifting weight of his body ripped another section of brush loose from its base in the rock.

The question was: could he pull himself onto the ledge before the brush gave way completely?

The robot was closer—much closer—making ponderous progress down the sharply angled face of the cliff. Soon he would be able to reach this man-thing. Soon.

Logan had swung his body to a point where he was finally able to get a grip on the ledge. Releasing the brush, he clawed his way up, levering his bruised body onto the narrow rock shelf.

But the robot was almost there—having lowered one metal leg to the ledge.

Logan twisted, pressing his back into the rock face for support, and kicked out with all his remaining strength at the thick metal limb of the machine.

The creature's leg slipped off!

For a long moment the robot swayed on one leg, grasping at the rooted brush with its single, steel-fingered hand.

"Not permitted," it said—and tumbled backward, past Logan, falling straight toward the sea, twisting, its metallic body sun-flashing as it arced downward, faster, to smash itself into metal death on the sea rocks below.

BAY OF DRAGONS

"All right, damn you, here's what you wanted!"

With a pale smile, Kirov accepted the Gun. The weapon looked outsize and unwieldy in his small hands as he sighted along its barrel, examined its smooth pearl grip. His smile faded. "But I cannot fire it! This Gun is unloaded! You have not met the terms of our agreement."

In a single stride, Logan closed the distance between them to grab the startled technician by the front of his uniform, pulling him close. His eyes burned into Kirov; his voice was iron. "The ammopac went into the sea. With the robot. I couldn't do anything to stop it. You asked for a Gun and I brought you one. *That* was our agreement, and you'd better live up to your end of it. If not, little man, I'll break you like a rotten stick!"

Logan released him, and Kirov fell back, shaken, lips trembling. He looked across the main living room of his unit at Jessica, who was glaring at him.

"Logan's right," she said. "You didn't mention any ammopac. You just asked for a Gun. And he brought it. He risked his *life* to bring it!"

Kirov raised a placating hand. "Very well," he murmured, attempting to regain his composure. He adjusted his wrinkled uniform. "I'll keep my end of the agreement. I shall program your new identities into the computer during tomorrow's workshift."

"We'll stay here tonight," Logan said to Jess. "By tomorrow, with any luck, I'll be talking to Francis."

Indeed, Kirov 2 kept his word—allowing Logan and Jessica to leave Moscow by mazecar the following afternoon as Treven 15, a New Chicago bodyjewel merchant, and his pairup, Jaci 3, a firewalker in the Angeles Arcade.

Kirov had seen to it that the Prestor databank was totally erased. When Federal authorities ran a trace on the bogus CIC inspector and Gun thief, Prestor 8, they learned nothing.

And within twenty-four hours, Kirov himself could not recall anyone named Prestor or Logan or Jessica or Treven or Jaci. He resumed his gray, uneventful life as a computer tech, wondering, from time to time, how he had come to possess a Sandman's Gun.

Kirov 2 never reported having the weapon because he knew that such a disclosure could lead to serious trouble. The Gun frightened him.

He finally buried it one night, very late, in the garden behind his unit.

At Angeles Complex, they left the maze, taking a belt up to the Wilshire sector. They had obtained appropriate clothing before leaving Moscow, but no physical alterations had been made in either of them. A facechange in a New You was totally impractical, since the idea was to prove themselves innocent of Phedra's charge. Thus, they risked recognition, particularly by Sandmen who knew Logan. His arrest would be the talk of DS Headquarters. Also, his face was known to many citizens, as it had been to Jessica. Almost anyone could stop him, point him out.

Yet it was essential that he reach his lifeunit.

"At least there's no active search for us," Logan told Jess. "As far as the Federal Police are concerned, we died on the Serengeti."

"But if we're scanned, our IDs may not hold," Jess reminded him. "Kirov is blocking for us—but that *can* be bypassed."

"So we don't get caught." Logan smiled.

They moved leisurely through the crowds; hurried movement attracted attention.

"Sandman!" hissed Jess at Logan's ear. "Just turned in our direction."

"Keep walking. Don't do anything," said Logan tightly.

The DS man was young and intense; his mind was on the runner ahead of him. Female. And she was clever. Giving him a good hunt. Exciting! His fingers touched the holstered Gun at his belt. Should be able to homer her before she reaches Arcade. My first solo kill!

He passed Logan and Jess without a glance.

Now they entered the Wilshire threemile, Logan's unit, taking a riser to the ninth level, moving quickly down the bright, high-ceilinged corridor.

Logan had kept Phedra's key, had hidden it on a corridor ledge before he left for duty on that first morning, figuring it might be wise to have it there in case of emergency. Now that decision paid off as he found the ledge and recovered the silver slotkey.

At his unit he tried the key, but the door refused to yield. A recorded voice informed them: "This life-unit has been sealed by Federal Police. There is no admission. Repeat: there is no admission."

Jess frowned, drew a harried breath. "What now?"

"We break the seal," said Logan. "I've broken them before."

"Without triggering the unit alarm?"

"There's no way to avoid that."

"But, Logan—they'll be here in less than a *minute* after that seal's broken!"

"Less than a minute is all I need," he said. And broke the seal.

The door opened and they hurried inside. No sound. The Federal alarm was silent but, in his mind, Logan could hear it screaming! Five seconds gone . . .

At the unit intercom he keyed in the number Francis had left with him.

"But you *know* he's not at his unit," Jess protested.

Ten seconds . . .

"His faxtape is," said Logan, waiting for the relay

pickup to engage. "Every DS man on freetime is required to leave his basic world location on a tape. And that's all I need."

Twenty seconds . . .

With the relay engaged, he ran in the faxcode numbers. Instantly, the gaunt Sandman's image filled the screen.

"Dragon Bay, Jamaica," said Francis.

Logan smiled, killing the relay.

They exited the unit building with ten seconds to spare.

"Identities!"

They were on the Wilshire platform, ready to board an express car, when two Federal officers stopped them.

Logan scowled at the two men, and continued to nudge Jess toward the car. An officer stepped between them on the boarding ramp.

"I'm Treven 15," snapped Logan, his tone officious and hard-edged, "and I have an important appointment in New Chicago. Treven Jewelworks—you've heard of me."

"Afraid not," said the officer who was blocking them.

"Identities!" repeated the second officer.

Sighing in obvious disgust, Logan dug into his traveltunic, removed a foilcard, and handed it over. The first officer took Jessica's card.

"We'll have to ask you to follow us," said the first officer.

"But why?" Jessica asked.

"We need to run a board check," replied the officer. "There's been a unit break-in, and we have a sight report that a man and woman fitting your description were seen leaving the building."

They were taken to a scanroom at the far end of the platform, where their cards were board-slotted.

"Please step inside. This won't take long."

Logan entered first, standing alone in the small chamber, telling himself: Steady, don't panic, this will be all right. Kirov's an expert. He's controlling the board. We'll get through this.

A light clicked on; the door released itself and Logan stepped out as Jessica entered. Her eyes were down; she looked nervous. Logan pressed her arm.

Within five minutes they were on a mazecar headed for the West Indies.

"Kirov kept his word," said Logan as they cleared the Angeles Complex in a bulleting rush. "He's giving us the time we need."

Jessica smiled. A tired smile. Her face was drawn, the skin taut across her cheeks.

"So now we find Francis," she said.

"Right." Logan nodded as the tunnel swept past them in a silver blur. "We find Francis."

South under Mexico, east through Guatemala into the Caribbean—to the West Indies and Jamaica, slowing as they moved beneath the island's girdling coral reef to the platform stop at New Port Royal. Since the island jungles had once provided a haven for runners, all incoming visitors were required to register with Jamaica CenControl.

"How long did Kirov say he could hold the cross-check?" asked Jess as they moved down the processing line.

"Six hours maximum," said Logan. "It's going to be close."

The computer cleared them.

"Citizen Treven . . . citizen Jaci . . . our island welcomes you!" said the dark-skinned port official, handing them their foilcards. "Please enjoy yourselves. As we say on the island, 'may the Undertaker's Wind blow all troubles away!'"

Back at the platform, armed with ID clearance, they boarded a local mazecar for the twenty-mile cross-island jump under the Blue Mountains to Dragon Bay on the rugged north coast, emerging into a blaze of color and lush tropical growth. An easy-flowing tradewind from the Caribbean stirred fern and bamboo, juniper and satinwood. Frigate birds skimmed the

white dazzle of beach, and immense Jamaican butter-
flies flashed their rainbow wings.

"The air's so clean," said Jess. "They say the
tradewinds never stop." She shaded her eyes against
the glare of white sand. "It's really lovely here . . . unspoiled."

"No part of this world's unspoiled," said Logan,
looking at the red crystal alive in his right palm. "Ask
a runner how unspoiled Jamaica is. This island's a potential deathtrap. If we don't find Francis, and soon,
we may never leave it."

"Where do we look for him?"

"He'll be hunting," said Logan. "Francis likes to
hunt."

"Dragon, mon! He hunt the big dragon!"

"Barracuda," Logan said to Jess. "The dragon of
the sea. Extremely difficult to catch."

"Oh, yes, mon!" The club attendant nodded his
dark, smooth-skinned head. "They like catch *you*.
'Cuda eat many hunters. Very . . ." he smiled broadly,
winking at Logan, "difficult."

The island clubroom was festooned with undersea
gear—from ancient metal diving helmets to modern
laserspears. Photos of myriad sea life crowded the
walls—and a large manta ray, fully extended, floated
above the main doorway, looking all too lifelike.

Logan checked the huntboard. Francis was logged
out as a solo.

When Logan asked about this, the attendant
shook his head. "Mon, you friend not wise," he said.
"*Nobody* hunt alone! Not here, mon. Never alone
here."

Logan wasn't surprised; it was characteristic of
Francis to ignore the dangers of a solo undersea hunt.

"What's he using?" Logan asked.

"He got a cat. Long range. Gone for long time."

"*How* long?"

"Long time now," said the attendant. He flashed
his wide smile again. His tone was musical, full of
secret mirth. "Many come here, hunt 'cuda. Not all
come back."

"I'm going after him," said Logan flatly.

Jess looked concerned. She put aside a shell she'd been holding. "You heard what he said about going out alone. I don't like your going out after him alone."

"I can handle it."

"I think you should wait. He'll be back . . . probably on the way right now."

"Or he could be in trouble right now," said Logan. "I've got to find him. If he's in trouble," and he looked at her steadily, *"we're* in trouble."

"Undertaker Wind blow all trouble away!" said the attendant.

And against the darkly burnished skin of his cheeks, his mocking white smile dazzled like beachsand.

THE SWIMMING DEATH

It was a world of cerulean blues, deep-velvet purples, inked greens, of wide brainstone coral cliffs and deep-bottomed troughs where the sea turned black in the chartless depths—a world of eel and octopus and squid, of the soldier crab and the loggerhead turtle, of jeweled angelfish, gliding manta rays, and great blue marlin. The majestic whale shared these rich Jamaican waters with the pulsating jellyfish—and the voracious shark, as old as time itself, prowled here in the daggered dark of the Caribbean.

Logan rode an open-cockpit two-man Seacat, swift and highly maneuverable, a sleek deep-water vehicle equipped with probing pinbeam lights and a stern-mounted minicannon powerful enough to penetrate any undersea obstacle.

He wore full lightweight bodyarmor, developed by Jamaican hunters to provide maximum protection against shark and barracuda.

"Within limits, of course," the outfitter had warned him as he'd donned the armored suit. "Some of these fellows can swallow you whole!"

"How strong is it?" Logan had asked.

"It's designed to withstand an ordinary slash attack—which will give you a chance to use the cannon if you have to." The outfitter, whose face bore a scar from chin to forehead, looked at him scornfully. "Not very sporting, though. Idea is to use a trank pistol on the fellow, then bring him in unmarked."

The tranquilizer was strong enough to put any barracuda to sleep—but then the problem became: how to net him to the Seacat and haul him in before his fellow denizens, sensing his lifeless state, tore him apart for lunch!

And me along with him, thought Logan. But of course he had no intention of netting a 'cuda; he was searching every trough and coral valley for Francis, pinbeaming the sea floor, powering the cat through masses of clinging sealace, over encrusted rocks, darting his light into the mouths of caves. . . .

Where were the dragons?

He saw several sharks; a manta rippled over him like a great shadowed blanket; a startled octopus unfurled like a dark flower from the lee of a sunken boulder; a fat trunkback turtle paddled by in lazy unconcern, ignoring this bizarre vehicle and the armored man who rode it.

But nowhere did Logan encounter barracuda. Perhaps by now they were wary of hunters; perhaps they avoided these sharp-snouted Seacats with their nets and lights and weapons.

But, eventually, Logan knew, he would find them. Or they would find him.

Jessica hated being left behind at the clubhouse. She had asked to go with him, but Logan had refused. Too dangerous, he'd insisted. She had no undersea experience, which might prove disastrous in case of emergency. He must go alone. Wait. Just wait. He'd be back with Francis.

She forced calmness upon herself; she tried to read one of the seahunt publications, but could not sit still. She ranged the hallways, glancing at the various trophies, at the mounted specimens of sea life, at weaponry new and old. She walked aimlessly into the equipment room, running her fingers along masks and fins and oiled tank fittings. The room sickened her: it smelled of brine and rubber and iodine.

She left without speaking to the outfitter, who stared at her.

What was wrong? *More* than her worries about Logan and the computer time running out and the rest of it, *more* than the tensions induced by their perilous situation. It was something else, something that threatened in a very personal way. She grew increasingly nervous and apprehensive.

And then she had the answer. So simple—and so horrible. Her shocked mind rejected it. No, can't be. Not yet. Not now.

No!

Standing alone in the club hallway, she slowly opened her right hand. In the center of her palm, the crystal timeflower was no longer a steady red. It pulsed like an angry heart: red-black . . . red-black . . . red-black. . . .

Jessica 6 was on Lastday.

The silo was a relic, built in the turbulent twentieth century, when one nation attempted to impress another with destructive power, when nuclear submarines patrolled the dark waters and bomb-laden aircraft rode global skies.

The submarines and the aircraft were gone, but the concrete-and-steel silos remained, deep-buried in land or under the seas, silent and long abandoned, their deadly missiles removed—stark reminders of a time when another kind of evil beyond Sandman and runner permeated the world, when war seemed ready

to bloom into monstrous atomic life, engulfing the
Earth in fire.

The tall, tubular structure loomed ahead, pinned
in Logan's lightbeam. He circled it in a wide arc, and
in jubilation found what he'd been searching for: a
Seacat, moored to the silo's lower section, swaying idly
in the surge of undersea currents.

I've found him! Francis *has* to be inside.

Logan quickly looped a holdchain over a project-
ing lichen-covered ladder along the near side of the
huge silo. His craft would be safe here. He removed a
spare breatherpac from the cat and snap-linked it to
his suit. Just to make certain he had ample oxygen in
case of trouble inside the silo.

He climbed the ladder to the massive overhead
entry hatch. The hatch doors had jammed open,
providing easy access.

Logan carried a portable pinbeamer to light his
way, and a laserspear was belted to his wrist. His wide
visorshield afforded a full field of vision.

He wore the armored suit comfortably, like a second skin, finding that it did not in any way hamper
normal body movement. The suit contained an
emergency mini-powerunit capable of limited indepen-
dent acceleration in case its wearer was injured and
could not propel himself through the water. Easily
enough power to get him back to the cat.

Logan kicked out with his lightweight, finned
diving boots, gliding swiftly downward, guided by the
pinbeam.

His light flashed across the owlish eyes of a large
blowfish, which instantly swelled into a defensive ball
of prickly white spines. A speckled moray eel whipped
past in the murky deep. As Logan angled down toward
the floor of the silo he passed a series of phosphores-
cent depth markers, the numerals still glowing faintly
in the thick green-black waters:

30'
60'
90'
120'

Iron-rung ladders spidered up the curved walls. He passed ruptured pipes and tubing choked with sea growth. A wire-cage elevator was frozen halfway between the upper hatch and the floor.

He swam toward it. Ran the beam inside. Empty.

Logan continued his descent, the suit equalizing body pressure, keeping the oxygen flow clear and steady. At last his boots touched the wide, debris-covered floor of the silo. Schools of curious suckerfish circled him as Logan swung the pinbeam toward a substantial, octagon-shaped structure in mid-floor.

Probably missile control. Francis could be in there.

Its door was open, and Logan swam through into a large instrumentation chamber. The room was a mass of dials, switches, control chairs, and computer decks, all heavily encrusted with sea life.

No sign of Francis. Logan felt a surge of disappointment. Of frustration. Where the hell *was* he?

He was about to leave the missile-control area when he noticed a second exit door to the far right. It had partially collapsed, and Logan barely managed to slip between the angled door edge and the floorbase.

Inside, his pinbeam traveled over tumbled equipment bins, a spillage of tools and electronic parts. Storage area. Nothing here.

But wait!

Something was moving to his left. A dark shape—just beyond a section of fallen bins . . .

Logan tensed, a hand on his speargun. If he surprised a manta down here, or a disgruntled octopus, he'd be in for a mean close-quarter attack. But the dark shape did not advance; it seemed unaffected by his presence.

He swam toward it, still warry, ducking under a section of twisted steel shelving to discover: Francis!

Logan beamed the Sandman's visorshield: eyes closed, mouth slack. Was he dead?

He studied the situation: Francis was wedged into a corner of the crowded storage area, his body jammed beneath a fallen portion of the ceiling. The moving shape Logan had seen from the doorway was the trapped Sandman's right arm, moving languidly up and down in the current created by Logan's passage.

Oxygen! He's probably out, Logan realized—quickly attaching the spare breatherpac, making the suit connection. He noted an immediate change in Francis: his eyelids fluttered open, his mouth gulping in the precious oxygen.

Logan unreeled a suit-to-suit intercom from a contact cylinder at his waist and plugged it into the Sandman's helmet.

"Francis, can you hear me?"

A nod. "Logan . . ."

"How badly hurt are you?"

The answering voice was strained; the words formed slowly: "Can't move . . . my legs. Other arm . . . think broken."

"What happened?"

"Curious . . . came in here to . . . look around . . . ceiling gave way . . . got trapped . . . oxygen gone. . . ."

"All right, I understand. I'll get you out."

"Can't move this bin . . . too heavy . . . jammed."

"I'll go back to the cat for a slicer. Cut you free. You've got enough oxygen now, so just hang on here till I get back."

Francis smiled faintly behind the visor. "I . . . won't be . . . going anywhere."

Logan broke the suit connection and swam for the exit.

The Seacat's S-6x penetration beam handunit, or "slicer," was extremely effective in lasering through the interlace of steel that held Francis pincered against the floor. Logan had almost succeeded in freeing the trapped Sandman when Francis suddenly jerked his right arm upward, directly into the path of the slice-beam. The laser cut deeply into his suit armor, slitting it from elbow to shoulder, before Francis was able to pull his arm away from the beam.

"What are you *doing?*" Logan yelled into the intercom.

"Muscle spasm," Francis replied. "Couldn't help
it." In shock, Francis watched his blood darkly cloud-
ing the water.

"It's bad," said Logan, checking the wound.
"Went right through your suit."

"I know . . . blood in the water. They'll come for
us."

"Are you able to swim?"

"No."

"I don't see a propulsion unit on your suit."

"Left it off," said Francis. "For lighter weight."

"We can both use mine," said Logan, slicing
through the final wedge of steel.

The job was done—but they were a long way
from safety.

Logan's suitunit propelled them steadily up
toward the silo's hatch in a froth of blood bubbles.

Francis was barely conscious, a dragging bulk for
Logan to maneuver; his arms and legs dangled, pup-
petlike, and through the intercom Logan could hear his
labored breathing.

The upper hatch loomed closer.

"We're almost there," said Logan. "Once we
reach the cat, I can get us away fast."

"Not . . . fast enough," said Francis weakly. "No
. . . chance." And his eyes closed.

"Hang on!"

"No . . . use . . . can't . . ."

He lapsed into coma.

At the hatch, Logan paused. Better check the
area before taking him out there, Logan told himself.
I'll leave Francis here, linked to the inner ladder; the
silo will protect him.

As Logan cleared the open hatch he drew back
his lips in a grimace of shock.

The dragons were here.

Barracuda.

A pack of them. Two dozen at least, circling the

tall silo in darting, nervous impatience, excited by the blood spoor.

The sea was filled with swimming death.

Logan choked back revulsion and fear. The laser-cannon would stop them. Get to a cat and use the cannon on them.

But the killer fish, with their ugly reptilian snouts and brute eyes, were between him and the Seacats—both of which were moored at the lower end of the silo.

Gripping a section of ladder outside the hatch, Logan attempted to clear his thoughts, pushing the fear away, mentally gearing himself for affirmative action. His mind raced:

Maybe I could fight my way through to one of the cats—but I can't leave Francis alone inside the silo. They'd go in after him, be on him before I could use the cannon; they'd tear him apart in seconds, and his damaged suit wouldn't stop them.

If I could just get *one* of them, then maybe . . .

Logan had the laserspear up, spring trigger at firing position. He had no expertise with a sea spear, had never fired one at an underwater target—and the erratic, darting 'cuda were extremely elusive.

Yet he must try.

He sighted on a huge, sheen-gray monster who seemed to be bolder than his fellows in that he swam much closer, in tighter circles, multirowed teeth shining whitely in his wide-hinged, killing jaw. Of all dangerous fish, the 'cuda was supreme in speed and deadliness—capable of cutting through the water at fifty miles per hour. Even its *tongue* had small, cruel teeth!

I'd rather face a school of shark than these devils, Logan thought, watching them glide closer. They don't fear me. They don't fear anything.

He triggered the speargun—and with a soft popping explosion the spearhead flashed toward the big gray devilfish.

And missed.

The point passed behind the 'cuda, lasering through a large sea boulder. Logan realized that he had failed to compensate for the angle of water-mass deflection. Aim ahead of the target, he told himself. Let the fish swim *into* the spearpoint.

Logan had fumbled a reload from his belt and was inserting it in the speargun when he was hit by the big gray. The barracuda's razored teeth raked furiously along the right side of his suit. The armor held—but he was thrown back against an upper edge of the silo, the speargun violently jolted from his grasp.

In desperation, he lunged for it, closing his gloved fingers around the trigger haft just as a second 'cuda struck at him, at his flippered left boot. The entire rubberized tip was sheared away, but the armor resisted penetration.

Logan swung the speargun back into firing position, noting that the pack was much closer now. They were tightening the death circle!

His second shot also missed, but by a much narrower margin. Logan had just one more reload for the weapon; the others were in the cat. If I miss this time . . .

Another monster charged him—but Logan dipped back behind the silo ladder as the 'cuda's teeth rang on the steel rung next to his head, scoring the metal.

Last shot. Must not miss. Look at them. Not afraid of me. Figure I can't hurt them. Lucky so far. Suit won't hold in mass attack. Closer to me. What's wrong? Taking too long to load. Hands not working. Breathing difficult. Oxygen giving out. Can't think. Weak. Coordination going . . .

Logan was on the edge of blackout; his breatherpac was nearly empty. He felt dizzy, uncertain; the moving 'cuda were gray-green blurs . . . wavering . . .

Focus! Concentrate!

The big gray was coming at him, obscene jaws gaped wide as Logan slowly brought up the speargun.

He fired, head-on, at the swift slicing deathshape.

The spearpoint flashed, imbedding itself in the barracuda's underslung jaw—lasering him neatly in half. A rush of spilled red flesh, an explosion of organs and entrails . . .

The pack went mad.

In a blood frenzy, they attacked their dying

leader, totally ignoring Logan as he tossed aside the empty speargun. Fighting to breathe, he pulled Francis out through the open hatch doors, activating the suit-propulsion unit.

They arrowed down toward Logan's moored Seacat.

Around them, in erupting crimson, the maddened fish struck wildly at one another, ripping and tearing.

Having reached the cat, Logan used his last breath to snap a fresh pac into his suit. The flowing rush of oxygen was incredibly sweet!

At the controls, with Francis locked into the cockpit next to him, he engaged full power. The Seacat jetted forward in a bubbled rush, while behind them, in the red froth of sea, the dragons clashed.

TIME OF RITUAL

"Gone?" Logan stared at the smiling man. "She *can't* be gone."

"I tell you, mon, she go!" He spread his dark hands. "Look all afraid. Ve-ry unhappy."

"She must have left some kind of message!"

The attendant frowned. "Message?" Then he smiled again, nodding with sudden vigor. Digging into his bushjacket, he withdrew a folded square of white paper. "Oh, sure, mon! I forget she leave this." His smile gleamed. "Fine message!"

Logan hurriedly unfolded the note.

Logan,
Francis can't help me now. No one can.
I'm on Lastday. Please don't try to find

me. Seeing you again would bring only
sadness. I hope you find *your* Jessica.

There was a four-word postscript:

I'm going to run.

"Hey, mon, she tell you where she go?"

"No," said Logan quietly, "she didn't tell me."

He walked from the room to the open patio.
Edged between dark clouds, the moon was hammered
gold. It cast a pale yellow glow on the night beach beyond the trees. A heavy odor of damp earth rose from
the jungle; rain was coming soon.

Logan walked through the trees toward the sea,
holding the note in his hand. On the beach he read it
once more . . . *I hope you find your Jessica* . . . then
dropped the paper into the damp sand. The reflecting
sea traced a faint wetness on his cheeks.

He'd lost them both—the two Jessicas. Both of
them. And he knew now, admitting it to himself for
the first time, that he loved the Jessica of this Earth
just as he continued to love the Jessica of his own
world. One lost in time and space, the other fleeing a
death she could never outrun.

Logan felt a sudden chill. The moon was buried
in a bulked mass of cloud. The jungle darkened.

And the rain began.

Francis took a day to heal. His right arm was
badly wrenched but not broken, and his other injuries
were minor. Within thirty-six hours he was in a
mazecar with Logan, heading back to California.

Logan was returning to Angeles Complex as a fu-
gitive in the custody of Francis, who assured him that
Phedra's story would soon be discredited.

"You saved my life at Dragon Bay," said Francis.
"Now I'll save yours."

"Have I lost Godbirth?" Logan asked him as the
mazecar bore them swiftly through deep-earth
darkness.

"No," said Francis. "You'll be eligible again once
the computer clears you." He placed a hand on Lo-

gan's shoulder. "Don't worry, old friend, we'll make Godbirth together. I guarantee it!"

And what of Jessica? Logan asked silently. What will happen to Jess when Lastday is over and the Sandmen go after her?

Don't think about her. You can't do anything to help her now—so quit thinking about her. Shut down your mind to her. She's gone. She never belonged to your world.

But I love her!

"You're going to be asked about that sister of Doyle's," Francis was saying to him. "And I'm personally curious. . . . Why *did* you get involved with her?"

"I didn't," said Logan flatly.

"Then how do you explain—"

"I was checking her out as a possible subversive when Phedra became jealous of us and manufactured that drug story." Logan spread his hands. "Then we were condemned to the Serengeti. When the Masai let us go, I was forced to take her along."

"Forced?"

"What else could I do? I had no reason to believe she'd run."

"Have any idea where she might be?"

"No," said Logan. "Does it matter?"

"Every runner matters."

"They aren't our problem anymore," said Logan. "Or have you forgotten?"

Francis smiled thinly. "It's hard to quit thinking like a Sandman."

"Sure," said Logan. "It takes a while."

Under pressure, at DS Headquarters, with Federal officers standing witness, Phedra confessed that she had lied about the drug. It was assumed that she had also planted the DD-15 on Logan that evening in Arcade.

"But I didn't," she protested.

"You lied before, you're lying again," said an officer.

"No, I'm telling the truth. I don't know how the Dust got into Logan's jacket."

"Take her away," the officer said. "She is to be executed."

"Clarify your full relationship with Jessica 6," directed the computer as Logan's interrogation continued.

"I've told you everything."

"It is to be repeated," said the computer.

And Logan repeated it all.

"Again," said the computer.

And Logan repeated it again.

Each answer was weighed and balanced and cross-checked for logic and accuracy.

"He is my friend. He is loyal to the system. He has never associated with subversives. His record with DS is exemplary. He is worthy of Godbirth." It was Francis, true to his promise, testifying on Logan's behalf.

The verdict was swift and positive: "Cleared of all charges."

That night Logan returned to DS Headquarters. He knew that Jessica's Lastday had ended. Her palmflower was now black. Death black. Sleep black.

Had she run?

The DS man in cenfile was young and in awe of Logan 3. His name was Bruce 11, and he had just graduated DS training, with his first hunt still ahead of him. The game was fresh and new and exciting to Bruce and he hoped, someday, to equal the proud kill-record of Logan 3. This was his secret, abiding goal—and he was delighted with the opportunity to serve this legendary Sandman. It was an honor.

What information, Logan asked him, did he have on a possible runner, female. Name: Jessica 6.

"Got her . . . she's on the board," said Bruce. "Flower blacked at 0612. She's somewhere in the Muir Woods area, near New Sanfrancisco."

Then she's run, just as she said she would, thought Logan. And into an area that is under water on my world, quake-sunken and lost. Nothing left but part of the bridge. Quake took all the rest—but here, now, Muir Woods is real and wild and Jess is running there, like a trapped animal before the hunters.

"Who's on the assignment?"

"Ummm, let's see . . ." Bruce checked a faxsheet. "Miles and Gregory have it." He smiled in assurance. "Both good men. They'll get her."

"I'm sure they will," said Logan. "I'd appreciate it if you'd forget I asked about her. I have my reasons."

"Certainly." Bruce nodded. "And . . . uh . . ."

Logan stared at him.

"I . . . just wanted to say . . . how much I respect you," the young man stammered. "Your record will be hard to match. I . . . envy you."

"You don't really know me," said Logan.

"I know you were a great Sandman," said Bruce, his voice rising. "No Sleep for you . . . You've earned it. You've earned Godbirth!"

And the young man's eyes shone with the word.

At shiftchange, when Miles 7 emerged from DS Headquarters, Logan was waiting for him near the hoverpad.

"I have a personal interest in the runner you hunted today," he told the DS man. "Jessica 6."

"What about her?" said Miles. He was bulky, hard-faced, a veteran. Logan's record didn't impress him. Nothing impressed Miles 7 except certain exotic favors he'd received at a local glasshouse.

Logan didn't want to ask the question that *had* to be asked. He drew in a breath, fighting to maintain a surface calm. The muscles in his cheeks were rigid.

"Is she dead?"

The DS veteran shrugged. "We had her totally blocked. No way out of the woods. She was locked on the scope—less than a mile ahead of us. But when we closed in . . ." He shrugged again. "Nothing."

"What do you mean?"

"You've heard of them. We all have. Runners who disappear. Females. They just vanish. That's the only word for it."

"She was gone when you closed in?"

"That's what I said. Gone. No trace of her."

"Maybe there is a Sanctuary," said Logan softly.

The DS man raised an eyebrow. "Sanctuary?" He stared at Logan. "What's that?"

With his fears for Jess eliminated (She wasn't homered! She may be alive somewhere on this Earth!) Logan gave himself over to Godbirth.

For Logan and Francis and the ten others in their group, it was the Time of Ritual. Their robot guide was tall and faceless and unapproachable and would answer no questions. He was there only to direct them; they must do precisely what he ordered.

They rode in tense silence through the maze.

Logan experienced a sense of renewed confidence. Against all odds, he had survived to make this journey. Perhaps he *could* uncover the world powerhead and defeat it; perhaps he *could* return to his own Earth, to Jess and their new son. . . .

The mazecar flashed through the long tunnels in a steady, humming surge, a glint of swift-running silver, moving. . . .

Where? To what global destination?

The platform they reached in final transit gave no hint of location. But as they left the maze they moved up into desert heat.

At ground level, they had their answer: upper Egypt. The eastern bank of the Nile.

They stepped from the maze exit into a stunning mass of carved granite, of shaped stone pillars and pylons and obelisks and massive courtyards open to sky and sun. They were in the Great Temple of Amon-Re, the Sun King, at Luxor, near Thebes, walking through a stone forest of immense drum columns that towered nearly seventy feet above their heads, each column alive with Egyptian hieroglyphs—an elaborate stone-cut history of this timeless land.

They were now allowed to ask their guide basic questions.

"Is this the Place of Miracles?" Logan asked.

"No," said the robot. "This is an area of prepara-

tion, where your bodies and minds will be cleansed—
so that you may be worthy to join the Gods."

"Bodies *and* minds," Logan remarked softly to
Francis. "That means they'll lift us, give us drugs."

"Don't judge things," Francis warned. "Just do
exactly what you're told to do. We're in other hands
now, Logan. We're into the ritual. Flow with it, don't
question it!"

Logan hated all drugs. As a Sandman, he had visited hallucimills when he'd been down, guilt-ridden,
when he had felt despair and depression. Drugs were
an escape from life, a weakness, a distortion of reality—the reflection of a sick society. But now he had to
accept the ritual. No choice. Don't question what happens, just let it happen. This is what you've been waiting for, fighting to reach. *Go* with it.

They were led down an avenue of cool stone, between tall rows of reclining ram-headed beasts with
shadowed eyes, past fountains that whispered in liquid
voices, to a wide courtyard dominated by a pool of
shining crystal edged in tinted limestone.

Here they undressed and bathed in the scented
waters.

In spungold sunrobes, they were led to the Place
of Meditation, a vast, stone-topped chamber forming
the heart of Amon-Re's temple. Surrounding them, lining the four walls, were rows of manlike beast-headed
Gods carved in black ebony.

The twelve were seated, in a loose circle, on satin
pillows. The floor of the chamber was covered with
soft furs, and the afternoon sunlight was muted to a
golden haze in this atmosphere of tranquillity.

Each of them was handed a small, delicately
wrought cup of scrolled silver—containing what the robot called "the elixir of divinity," designed to place
them in "a state of inner peace and receptivity."

Receptive to *what*? Logan wondered. According
to the aliens, he had been provided with a mindshield
against this type of mental preconditioning. Therefore,
no drug, however potent, could have a lasting effect on
him.

I'll go under, but I'll come out clean. I'm shielded against ultimate mental control.

Or *am* I?

Francis smiled, raising his cup. "To Godbirth!"

And they drank.

PAIN AND ANGUISH

Now they were out of Egypt, in a mazecar headed for Cape Steinbeck, to the rockets, and Francis was Ballard, which was perfectly normal, perfectly understandable, and Logan was glad it was over.

Jessica was waiting for him on board the rocket. Ballard had brought her there from Jamaica.

"She was running," said Ballard, old and tired, with the gray in his hair making him look older—but then, he'd lived a double lifetime. . . .

"Thank you for saving her," said Logan.

"That's my job. Saving people. That's what I'm here to do. As Francis I kill them and as Ballard I save them. We each have our job."

"I thought you were dead," Logan told him.

"Well, I'm here. I'm with you in this mazecar. That's proof of life, isn't it?"

"There's too much death," said Logan. "I'm glad you survived."

"You'll survive too, Logan," said the tired man. "You don't quit. You never give up. You'll survive."

The mazecar slotted into a platform and they climbed out.

They were at Steinbeck, at the edge of the Keys, and the muggy Florida heat assaulted them as they cleared the maze.

It was noon, and desperately hot. Serengeti heat.
The tarmac bubbled and steamed beneath Logan as he
walked. The raw smell of tar was in the air, and the
long plain ahead of them shimmered and danced.

"There, Logan! The rocket!"

Logan raised his head, blinking.

"She's on board, waiting for you. Jess is waiting!"

The rocket was tall and magnificent, glinting
against the horizon, a thing of power and grace and
beauty. A mountain of metal, a silver Kilimanjaro rising into baked blue sky.

Logan smiled. He would ride this great ship into
space, ride it home with Jess, to their son, to young
Jaq and Fennister and Mary-Mary and Jonath. . . .

No, Jonath was dead. Evans 9 had Gunned him
at Crazy Horse. Used a ripper on him.

"Here we are," said Ballard, standing with Logan
at the foot of the iron ladder that led to the open port.
"Better get aboard."

They shook hands firmly. "I owe you everything,"
said Logan. His voice was tight with emotion.

"Nonsense. You owe me nothing. *You* did it . . .
you survived. You'll never die, Logan. They can't kill
you. They tried, with their power and their Guns, but
you eluded them, outwitted them. You lived as others
died."

"Jonath wanted to live," said Logan.

"We *all* want to live. With you, we run, we survive."

"They killed Jaq. The Riders killed him."

"He lives in you. And in Jessica. A new Jaq
lives!"

Ballard made it all sound right. Simple and direct
and easy to understand. All of it easy. No mysteries.
No guilts. No losses.

"Come with us, Ballard! Home! To a better
Earth."

The gray man shook his head slowly. "I've got my
job to do here." he said quietly.

"And if they kill you?"

"Then I'll live in you," he said, smiling.

And Logan began climbing the ladder.

Upward, steeply upward, steel rung after steel rung after steel rung after steel rung . . .

The rocket was very tall, miles tall, and Logan had to climb all the way up to reach Jess. All the way.

A mile up, he paused. Jessica was waving to him from the open hatch, a tiny warm dot above him. He looked down, over his right shoulder—and Ballard was Francis, all in black, all in killing black, with the Gun shining, and with his skull-thin smile shining and his eyes dark, and shining in the sudden midnight that engulfed them, engulfed the Keys, the tall rocket, the ladder. . . .

Where was Jess now? Logan could no longer see her; the darkness was too thick, like dense smoke. His tongue tasted of rust and bile as he continued to climb. Rung after steel rung after steel rung after steel rung after steel rung . . .

How high now?

Three miles? Four?

Below him, Francis aimed the Gun. "Time to die, Logan," he said in a soft, venomous whisper. Logan heard him clearly.

"No, damn you, no!" And he began climbing faster.

Must outclimb the homer, he told himself. Because it's coming for me. He's fired it by now, and it's unfair. Totally unfair. He told me I'd live forever. He lied. No, not Ballard. He would never lie. It was Francis. You could never trust Francis. Keep it all straight in your mind. Don't get confused.

It's coming for me. As it came for the girl near the fence back at Angeles in that other world so long ago. Remember her? Oh, it came for her and she tried to run and it followed her along the fence and it took out her entire nervous system like bursting stars. Starflesh. Bursting.

Logan could feel it coming up through the heavy dark, slicing the night, fast, fast. . . .

Hurry! Rung after steel rung after steel rung after steel rung . . . climbing for Jess. Climbing for life.

There! He was at the hatch. He'd made it!

He reached the open port and in the fogged darkness he was pulled on board the ship.

The hatch slammed shut.

Saved! He'd outclimbed the homer!

Jessica was in his arms. Her lips were sweet. Her hair smelled of hyacinth and wild honey. Her eyes were shining with love, shining like the eyes of Francis.

She was Francis.

"There's no escape," the gaunt Sandman whispered, and his smile was a knife, cutting.

He fired the homer into Logan's stomach.

With the charge working in him, tearing him apart, with his nerves splitting, ripping, unraveling, he clawed open the hatch and jumped from the silo.

Into the jaws of the dragon . . . into the 'cuda's razored mouth.

And the dark gouted blood.

. . . drug . . . in the cup . . . making all this . . . must not let it . . . control me . . . . not . . . let it . . .

Francis stroked the girl's naked shoulder with gentle fingers. His voice was soft, his dark eyes filled with sadness. "She's so beautiful, Logan . . . so very, very beautiful."

"But why is she here?"

They were in the main databank report room at DS. The room was very quiet. All the boards were silent. No one else was there.

Just Logan, Francis, and the girl.

"I asked her to come here," said Francis. He reached out, tipped up her chin. "Open your eyes. Tell Logan your name."

The girl opened her eyes. She was sitting in front of the central feeder unit, her naked body illumined faintly by the banded rows of glowing circuit lights. The lights struck through her blond hair, creating filaments of glowing gold. Her full breasts stirred as she turned toward Logan.

"I'm Glinith," she said. "Glinith 21. And that's what I'll be very soon!" She giggled, holding out her right hand to him, palm up. "See!" The time-crystal was blinking.

"She's on Lastday," said Francis, stroking her night-dark hair. The lights of the board were smothered and trapped in this inked mane of full-spilling hair. "She'll be dead very soon."

"Very soon," echoed Glinith, and her hair was deep-crimson, flowing like soft fire to her waist.

Logan was alert, cat-nervous. Things were wrong in this room. Many wrong things here. "Why are the boards inactive?" he asked Francis.

"Simple." The gaunt man nodded. "All the runners are dead."

"All dead," echoed the girl. She extended her arms. "Take me, Logan. Sex me!"

"No." He shook his head. "Not now. Not here. It's all wrong here."

"I'll take her." Francis grinned, stripping his uniform. He lifted Glinith from the control chair, placing her gently on the polished black-marble floor.

Francis touched her breasts, spreading himself beside her on the cool marble. She ran her hands slowly over his naked chest, her hair gold now under the flickered lights.

Logan said, "I'm going."

"Where?" asked Francis, as the girl writhed beneath him. "Where is there to go?"

"Back to my unit."

"It's not there," Francis said, and the girl moaned softly as his body penetrated hers. "Nothing's out there, Logan. It's all here. Everything is *here*."

The girl sobbed, cried out in sharp release as Francis rolled away from her. Sweat glistened along his shoulders and back, a finely beaded mist. The sweat of cold passion.

Logan could not find the exit door.

Something was very wrong.

"Hand me my belt," said Francis.

The girl lay face down on the mirror-polished floor, breathing deeply.

Wrong.

Logan gave the belt to Francis, who unsnapped

the Gun holster. He removed the weapon. It pulsed in
molten heat against the girl's skin as Francis pressed
the long barrel into her lower spine.

"What are you doing?" Logan asked.

"Killing her," said Francis. "She's on black now."

And he triggered the Gun.

The nitro blew the girl apart.

    *. . . the drug is . . . what is this . . . doing to me
. . . wrong . . . twisted . . . I'll be all right . . . if I
. . . can . . . just . . .*

And Jessica stared at her mirror-imaged self.
"Why did you come here? Why come to me?"

"To tell you that Logan is dead," said Jess.
"Francis killed him. It was inevitable. No one can escape Francis."

"Did you love him?"

"Yes. As you did. We both loved him, and he
loved both of us. In many ways, to him, we were the
same person. Exactly alike."

"I'm not like you. I have a son."

"My flesh is yours."

"Not mine. No. You come from another world,"

"Bridged by space and time."

"But uncrossable. Each world separate. Each cut
off from the other."

"But I'm here. You see me."

"I see myself. The mirror self. Only me. Not you.
I'm alone here. And Jaq is dead."

Jessica was sobbing, holding the dead child
tightly, rocking his charred, lifeless body in an agony
of sorrow.

Beyond the lightless house, the dark empty bed of
the Potomac ran like an open wound past the hill. The
Riders were gone, but the blood was here. Here in this
house, this hallway, staining Jaq's blistered corpse.

"You've got to accept it," Logan told her.
"They've killed him and there's nothing we can do."

She looked up at Logan. "You were gone. I was
here alone with our son. Helpless against them. I

couldn't stop them." Her eyes burned at him. "Why weren't you here?"

"I was on another world," he told her. "Trapped there. I couldn't get back to you. I tried, but I couldn't."

Her face was cold, unforgiving. "Jaq is dead because of you. The Riders killed him because you weren't here when he needed you." Her tone was bitter. "I *hate* you, Logan! Hate you! Jaq is dead because of you!"

"No!" Logan was trying to make her understand. "I just couldn't . . . tried but . . . couldn't. . . .

. . . get back . . . can't get away from . . . but must . . . keep my mind . . . can't let them . . . take my . . . mind . . .

Logan sat up on the sweated pillow, staring at his hands. He had fisted them, and now his flexing fingers felt stiff and unreal. His skin was hot, flushed; it seemed too thinly stretched over the bones of his body. His muscles ached dully.

To his right, Francis was also coming out of the drug lift, as were others in the circle.

The robot guide faced them. "You have all experienced death and pain and personal anguish, but this was as expected. The elixir was meant to do this, to cleanse your minds of crippling emotions—to place you in a receptive state of calm inner peace."

Logan looked at the others. They were numbed, their eyes devoid of expression. The robot voice droned on and the figures in the circle listened, transfixed.

"Let me assure you that all pain and anguish is past now. Only brightness and joy await you. Stand up! Rise! It is time for me to guide you to the Place of Miracles."

The aliens had promised Logan immunity—and now he felt the numbing effects of the elixir draining from his mind. He was becoming fully alert again, aware of exactly what was happening to him and around him.

Not so with Francis and the others; their eyes

were glazed; they moved sluggishly, silently after the guide. The drug had them in its grip. They would believe what they were told to believe, see what they were told to see. . . .

Logan felt elated. Excitement roared through him. At last, after overcoming impossible odds, he was about to learn the secret of Godbirth.

THE GODBIRTH PROCESS

North, by sailjet, down the river to lower Egypt as the blue-green snake of water swells into the Nile Delta. Then, on foot, to the hot, broken plain of Giza in the Valley of Kings.

Standing with the others in the colossal shadow of the Sphinx, Logan was startled to realize that the Great Pyramid of Cheops was gone. In his world, he had visited it as a boy, and was familiar with the site. Now the ground was bare—simply an area of dusting yellow sand. Perhaps, on *this* Earth, the Pyramid had never been built.

Other groups had arrived, other Chosen Ones— DS men from various parts of the world, each group of a dozen led by an identical guide robot. The group members were silent—and from their numbed, listless attitude, it was obvious that they had all ingested the drug.

One of the robots, taking command, raised an arm for attention. "Let the tribute be revealed!"

The sand at the base of the Sphinx began sifting back from a wide slotdoor set into the desert; it slid open to reveal a rising platform of world treasures; here were dozens of massive, open-topped crates containing jeweled crowns, master paintings, rare coins, sculptures and artifacts from many countries. The late-afternoon sun caught their edges, icing them with gold, a spangled brightness that caused Logan to shade his eyes.

He marveled at these treasures. The Gods do all right for themselves, whoever they are! He glanced at Francis, who was standing near him, hands folded into his robe, eyes fixed on the robot leader. Waiting to jump when they pull the strings, Logan knew. No will of his own.

Logan shifted his attention back to the guide robot, placing his hands inside the sunrobe and dulling his expression. Remember to mimic the rest of them, he told himself. What they do *you* do!

The robot looked at the sky, spreading both arms in a wide gesture. "The Gods! They arrive in fire to bear you to Nirvana! Kneel. Prepare for their coming."

With the others, Logan dropped to his knees in the warm sand.

"The sacred cloud descends!" announced the robot solemnly as the sky began to darken.

An immense cloud was spreading over the area, casting its shadow over all of them.

It's artificial, Logan realized. This is no "sacred cloud"—it's smoke, being piped down from a source above to set the scene.

Logan tented his hands in an attitude of prayer, following the example of the robots. A good act so far, he thought. The "Gods" should be here anytime now.

A roaring filled the sky, and Logan could see dozens of fiery forms descending through the smoke.

"Let the Gods be welcomed!" cried the robot.

The Chosen Ones bowed low as a host of helmeted figures burst through the cloud, alive with fire and light. The roaring increased, and the sand whipped up in swirling yellow ribbons.

Bent forward with the others in supplication, Logan had it figured: the "Gods" were wearing antigrav flying belts, and were costumed in light-jeweled uniforms set to dazzle the eye—particularly the *drugged* eye.

To Francis and the other mind-numbed DS men, these fiery figures would indeed appear godlike and miraculous.

One of the helmeted figures landed beside Logan and looped a flybelt around his waist.

"Nirvana awaits you!" announced the God-figure, and Logan felt himself lifted into the sky by the jetbelt, the God riding at his side, holding his arm, guiding their upward journey.

Each of the Chosen Ones was thus borne up by a helmeted figure while other "Gods" were attaching antigrav belts to the crated treasures on the platform.

Far above, a tremendous white cloud filled the sky, unmoving, frozen there in space, a visually impenetrable mass toward which they flew.

It doesn't move because it's not a cloud, thought Logan. Another trick effect—some type of artificial substance placed there to mask whatever's behind it.

The white mass flowed around them like heavy fog, so thick that Logan was unable to see the figure directly beside him; he felt weightless, bodiless, caught up in a white dream. . . .

And then they broke through, into calm blue sky, and Logan beheld the cloud's secret.

Nirvana.

A gigantic city, riding above the Earth in glittering majesty, of a size to stun the senses, its great domes golden with sun, its vast array of buildings rising in multilevel profusion, tiers and terraces and clustered towers, with swift sky vehicles threading them like silver-stitching needles.

They entered the sky city through a slidehatch in the lower section that housed Nirvana's immense solar engines. As a climbway took them to the city's interior, Logan was careful to maintain his pose of drugged serenity. Around him, the other DS men moved, trancelike, to the orders of the helmeted God who now directed them.

At top level, they stepped onto a transbelt that took them to one of the domed buildings within the city's central core. Along their route, the streets were empty, which Logan found strange for a city of this size. Where were the people? Who lived here in these high towers? And who controlled it all? What was the source of "Godpower" behind this man-made Nirvana?

Inside the building, they were seated on a long wallcouch, the only item of furniture within the glass-walled, rectangular room.

Their guide removed his helmet, revealing himself as an ex-Sandman named Halpern. "I'm a God now," Halpern told them. "Soon you will also be Gods—once the ritual has been completed."

The man spoke in a leaden voice, with his words oddly spaced, and Logan realized that Halpern, like the others, was under a form of mind control. The blind leading the blind!

Logan glanced directly at Francis, who was seated farther along the couch, attempting to make eye contact—but the gaunt Sandman was blank-faced; there was no flicker of recognition in his fixed stare.

The chamber was darkening; descending alum curtains were cutting the light, closing out the glassed sides of the room.

"Now," said Halpern, "the time has come for you to meet our Master, who shall share Godpower with you, who shall initiate your birth as Immortals . . . the God of Gods . . . Sturdivent!"

In a shimmer of blue fire, a giant skull materialized at the center of the room. The bones took on flesh—and a face of awesome power shaped itself before them, a wide, ridged face with thrusting cheekbones, a down-slashed nose, and haunting eyes that blazed hypnotically from the floating head.

Tri-dim effect, Logan knew. This dramatic materialization was as phony as the cloud beneath the city, another clever display of theatrics designed to impart a supernatural aspect to the proceedings.

He puts on a good show, Logan admitted; a first-class act. And Logan knew, that if the aliens had not provided shielding, he'd be as mesmerized by all this as the other DS men around him.

The floating head began to speak in a deep, vibrating voice, electronically augmented to achieve max-

imum power. Each word vibrated directly into the
minds of the assembled Chosen Ones.

"From this moment forward, you are, each of
you, elevated beyond man, to the status of Immortals.
I, Sturdivent, deem it so. I, Sturdivent, declare that you
are now of the brotherhood of Gods. You are herewith
reborn in my name!"

As he spoke these words, the blazing eyes, combined with his compelling voice, created a total hypnotic effect. Logan could see that every DS man in the
room was under Sturdivent's control.

Their minds belonged to him.

The words flowed on: "Henceforth, you will serve
me as my personal Gods here in Nirvana and on Earth
as I bid you." A pause. The eyes raking, cutting into
them. "Say that you will serve me—that you will
obey!"

"We will obey," intoned Francis and the others.
Logan, too, repeated the words, but with an inner contempt for such blatant manipulation.

"You will serve only Sturdivent!"

"We will serve only Sturdivent."

"I am your Master in all things. I am your world.
In me, you live forever. Through the power of Sturdivent!"

"Sturdivent . . . Sturdivent . . . Sturdivent . . ."
A rising chant, as they repeated his name over and
over in mindless litany.

Slowly, the Godhead dissolved, fire-flickered into
darkness.

At last, Logan knew the ironic truth about Godbirth.

Godbirth was slavery.

That night each man was assigned a lifeunit
within the core section of the city, in one of the central
towers. The units were functional, but basically sterile—gray and lifeless. Their main feature was a full-
wall screen, facing the flowbed, which, Logan quickly
realized, served a dual purpose: to keep them under
observation during sleep, and to maintain primary
mental control. With its swirling shapes and shifting

color patterns, the screen acted as yet another form of hypnosis.

He was exhausted. The flowbed took him, shaping itself to his body, soothing him toward sleep. As he closed his eyes, troubling questions formed: What is Sturdivent's ultimate plan in furthering the Godbirth process? He obviously controls the computers of the world, and has built this drug-based religion for his own purposes. But what, exactly, *are* these purposes, and how can he be stopped? What can I do, alone, against an entire city of mind-slaves?

Logan was finally here, at this second Earth's main powerhead, but he had no plan, no way to achieve his impossible mission.

The eyes of Sturdivent filled the screen; his voice was rich and lulling: "Sleep now . . . sleep . . . sleep . . ."

Logan allowed the voice to calm him, to ease him toward oblivion.

He slept.

WITH THE MASTER

Morning sun was warm against Logan's face when a guide robot awakened him.

"You have been summoned," the robot said.

'Where . . . am I to go?' Logan asked, remembering to keep his voice at a dulled monotone.

"The Master has sent for you," said the robot.

After a needleshower and fresh clothing (softfit boots and bodysuit), Logan followed the guide to a small sky vehicle waiting on the tower's upper level.

"This machine will take you to the Master. Please step inside."

Logan entered, seating himself—and the skycraft took flight, soaring soundlessly above the wide, deserted avenues of the city.

I'm probably being watched, even here, alone in this thing, thought Logan. What does Sturdivent want with me? Maybe he knows I've been faking. This could be an arrest! What about Francis and the others? Have they been summoned?

The craft angled down, settling like a dropped leaf to the roof of a split-terraced building of impressive size at the city's core.

Logan exited to a belt that took him through an entrance door into a long hallway, smelling of cool metal, where another guide robot met him.

"Follow me," directed the robot.

He was led down a series of intersecting corridors that gave way eventually to a vast court. Logan marveled. Here, facing him in all its magnificence, was the missing Pyramid of Cheops—having been taken up, stone by immense stone, from the desert floor in the Valley of Kings, to be assembled here for the pleasure of the Master. Here, too, Logan recognized Michelangelo's masterwork of David—one of countless world treasures collected from every part of the globe, the wealth of Earth, paid as tribute to the Gods, but actually taken into the personal possession of Sturdivent.

At least Logan was not alone here. Other DS men were filing into the courtyard, a dozen in all. Francis was among them, still under the drug, his face stony and remote. He looked at Logan with dead eyes; there was no rapport between the two ex-Sandmen.

A robot stepped toward them, indicating that they should follow.

Back to the corridors. Down a long slipway into the heart of the building. Along another hall. Very dim lighting. Silent. Sepulchral. A drifting odor of incense. An atmosphere befitting the God of Gods . . .

Then—a tall door filigreed in silver. It fell back with the faintest hiss of sound, and the robot nodded them forward. "He awaits you."

Were they to meet him now, the real Sturdivent—or would this be another of his clever manifestations?

They stepped inside.

The room sparkled with crown jewels, reflected in the gleam of oiled canvas along the walls, paintings by the giants of each era. Greek sculptures flanked a huge desk of veined marble. At this desk, this throne, sat the Godhead, the Master, the supreme ruler of Nirvana.

Sturdivent.

Not a God, a *man*. He stood to greet them, tall, massive of shoulder, deep-chested, his corded legs booted in silver, his tunic black velvet stitched in crimson, his fingers ringed in diamonds, a circlet of jade at his cat-muscled waist.

"Welcome to my city," he said, looking at each of them with eyes that possessed and dominated. Logan felt the heat of these eyes move across his body. Never had he faced a more compelling presence. A man, yes, but a God in bearing and stature.

Sturdivent directed them to be seated, in a half-circle facing him, in carved oak chairs of classic design.

The Master resumed his place at the desk, his eyes never leaving their faces. "In each grouping at Godbirth," he said, "I select a dozen unique individuals. This selection is carefully made."

His voice was deep, as magnetic as the man himself. It did not require amplification; the tone was riveting.

"You have, each of you, proven your worth as superior Sandmen—the pride of your Complex. Francis and Logan from California . . . Beaudry and Lefforts from Paris . . . Hennessey and Collins from London . . . all of you, from Tokyo, Berlin, the Netherlands—outstanding in your areas."

Again he measured them with his eyes, and Logan felt the power of this man; it was as if Sturdivent could look into his soul, as if he could read Logan's deepest thoughts.

"From this city I now control the Central Computer," he told them. "The treasures of this world are mine—but they are not enough. To build power I have had to use subterfuge, remaining cut off from Earth, in isolation here. But this will soon end." His eyes continued to sweep them, hold them. "With my Gods, with you and others like you as leaders in this mass action, I plan to assume personal rule on this planet. The stage is now set. We will strike from the sky at key points around the globe, eliminating the nominal base of authority . . . DS . . . Federal Police . . . and after we have established total control I will suitably reward each of you. You will rule Earth with me."

Replacing one form of corruption with another, thought Logan. As Gant had hoped to do at Crazy Horse. Logan glanced covertly at the others. They were impassive. Nothing Sturdivent told them elicited an emotional response. They would obey his orders without question.

Sturdivent swung his gaze to Logan as he opened a drawer in the desk. He withdrew a heat-penetration handgun, placed the burnweapon on the desktop, and leaned forward.

"Take it," he said to Logan.

Logan walked to the desk and picked up the weapon, waiting for Sturdivent to speak again.

The Master rose and walked toward the group. "Any one of you must be prepared to die for me at a given command," he said. Sturdivent placed his ringed hand on the shoulder of a husky, thick-necked DS man.

"Stand up, Hennessey 4," he said quietly.

The big man obeyed.

Sturdivent turned, smiling, to Logan. "Burn him."

Logan found it almost impossible to maintain outer coolness, to appear indifferent in the wake of such an order.

Do it, he told himself harshly. Don't let your face betray you. Stay cold, emotionless. Don't think about it, just do it. Hennessey wouldn't be here, in this room, in this city, if he wasn't a notorious killer. He's Gunned dozens of runners—and he deserves to die.

You've killed before. You can kill again.

And if I don't, Logan told himself, *I'll* be the one to die. I'll never live to see my son. . . .

Do it!

Hennessey regarded him with flat, opaque eyes. No fear. No recognition of impending death.

Logan raised the burnweapon.

And fired.

The heat charge struck the big man at shoulder level and the body exploded into ruin, toppling to the chamber floor. A thin gray smokemist hovered above the charred corpse as Logan calmly returned Sturdivent's weapon to the desktop.

"Thank you, Logan 3," said the Master, turning from the group and walking out of the room.

"You may leave now," said the guide robot.

Logan did not look back at Hennessey's body as they exited the jeweled chamber.

THE DREAM QUARTER

That night: a celebration.

"To welcome you and the other new Gods," the unit robot told them as the skycity pulsed with light. The radiant domes and illuminated towers bathed them in brightness as a flowbelt took their group along a central passway toward the Palace of Celebration.

Logan felt numb; the kill he'd been forced to perform for Sturdivent left him depressed and enervated. He regretted killing Hennessey. I should have turned the gun on Sturdivent, Logan told himself; *he's* the one I must destroy to end this thing.

But the robots would have burned me down if I'd attempted it. His guards would never have allowed me to kill him. You don't shoot God with his own gun. I'll have to find another way to deal with him.

Another way . . .

At the Palace of Celebration—an open-court, triple-tier structure in the heart of the city—Logan was impressed with the number of "Gods" in attendance. Sturdivent's plan for world domination seemed sure to succeed; here were gathered over a thousand ex-Sandmen, best of the best, each of them pledged body and soul to Sturdivent's service.

The new Gods were toasted with wine, and formally welcomed to Sturdivent's kingdom by the DS men of senior status. To Logan, the celebration was a travesty and a perversion—since all its participants remained in a mind-drugged state. They ate and drank and conversed in emotionless, mechanistic fashion. And in the midst of such a distorted celebration Logan's depression deepened.

Suddenly Francis was beside him, a wineflask in hand. He offered the wine to Logan. "Safe to drink it," he said quietly. "It's not drugged."

Logan was startled. "You're—"

"Normal." Francis nodded. "Their drug didn't affect me. I've been able to resist it. But I wasn't sure about you. Not until earlier today—when you killed the Sandman."

"How could you tell I wasn't drugged?"

"I was observing you closely," said Francis. "You hesitated for a fraction of a second just before you fired. No one else in that room would have hesitated. That's when I was sure of you."

"Did Sturdivent notice my hesitation?"

"I'm certain he didn't. He's too secure in his own massive egocentricity. After all, you *did* kill the man. That was enough for Sturdivent. Your act was foolproof."

"Well, you haven't been doing so bad yourself," said Logan. "I was convinced you were like all the others. How did you overcome the drug?"

Francis smiled. "We're both strong men, Logan—stronger than Sturdivent counted on. The elixir produced hallucinations, but I came out of them—just as you did. We're special, Logan. Two of a kind."

But, Logan responded silently, I had the shielding, and you didn't. How did you manage to do what no other DS man has done?

"We can work together," Francis was saying. "Since we're among Sturdivent's 'elite' we have much more freedom and flexibility than the others."

"How do you know Sturdivent isn't having us watched?"

"Oh, he is—but superficially. At night, in our units. Basic wallscreen observation. But we're free to roam the city. Without observation."

"You've done it . . . checked it out?"

"Absolutely. No one's bothered me or followed me or questioned me. We're safe from suspicion so long as we act like the others."

"What about the robots?"

"They've been programmed to leave us alone unless we violate a basic city-law," said Francis. "If we're careful, they'll be no problem." He looked hard at Logan. "The main thing is, Sturdivent must be stopped. He's out to destroy DS."

Logan's depression lifted; he was no longer alone. Francis, for whatever his reasons, was going to help him accomplish the aliens' mission. They would work together again as a team. And together, on this Earth or Logan's, they had been unbeatable. If Sturdivent could be stopped, they'd stop him.

"Do you have a plan?" asked Logan.

"First, we have to escape the city," said Francis. "And I think I've found a way out. If we can steal two antigrav units we can exit through the Dream Quarter."

"What's that?"

"At the far end of the city. Come on, I'll show you. But keep the act up. Move slowly. And don't say anything to me on the street."

"Right." Logan nodded.

They crossed the wide night city, riding the belts in silence, allowing the domed buildings to flow past them in luminous procession.

Logan had been mentally charting the days, sunrise to sunset, since the aliens had sent him to Earth.

He was running out of time. Less than twenty-four hours remained before he'd be abandoned here forever, with no hope of returning to his home world.

To Jess and Fennister and Mary-Mary, to the Wilderness People at Maincamp, I'm already dead, thought Logan. Lost in the sky, gone without a trace. He knew that Jess would be grieving for him, desolate that Jaq would never know his father. Therefore, one thought was a twisting knife in Logan's mind, repeating itself over and over: I must get back to them . . . I must get back to them. . . .

Francis stepped from the belt, Logan following. They waited in shadow until a unit robot had passed, then entered a squat copper-colored utility structure built over a complex cross-hatching of wide metalloid struts.

"These support the solar powerhousing," said Francis when they were inside. He tapped one of the struts. "This one leads directly to a booster cone that has a utility-repair exit port. Once we have the flybelts, we can leave through the port without attracting attention. Sturdivent will never know we're gone."

"When we're out—what then?"

"We alert central DS to the truth about what's going on up here," said Francis. "Once we've shattered the Godbirth myth, with a few squads of armed DS in skybugs we can knock out this city and finish Sturdivent."

Logan was uncertain. "And what happens to all the brainwashed ex-Sandmen?"

"They die, of course," said Francis flatly. "And the Dreamers with them."

"Dreamers?"

"That's why they call this area the Dream Quarter. Because of them."

"You know a lot that I don't," said Logan. "Who are these Dreamers?"

"Sturdivent's special slaves," said Francis. "Kept down here away from the other Gods. One of the robots told me about them."

"Are they ex-DS?"

"Maybe. Don't know."

"I want to see them," said Logan.

"But, Logan—"

"Do you know where they are?"

"Yes, but it might be dangerous," Francis objected. "We can't afford to risk—"

"I want to see them," Logan repeated.

They did not have far to go. The Dreamers were housed in a subterranean section of a building directly adjoining the main utility block.

"What about guards?" Logan asked in a whisper as they moved along a narrow metal walkway leading to the ventilation tunnel.

"According to the robot, they keep two. One inside with the Dreamers, and another outside the door. We can avoid them if we use the tunnel."

At the ventilation shaft, they loosened a wallplate, pried it off, and quickly climbed inside. The shaft tunnel was high enough to permit them to move rapidly through it in a running half-crouch.

"What we're doing is crazy, Logan. We should be using this time to prepare our exit from the city. Why are you so determined to do this?"

"Because I have a hunch about the Dreamers," said Logan. "I don't think they're DS men."

And they weren't.

"Women!" marveled Francis, peering down at the dreaming figures. The ventilation tunnel passed directly through the large, dim-lit Dream Chamber—affording Logan and Francis a clear view of the Dreamers below.

Fifty of them. Lying in easy-breathing rows of five, their nude bodies in fetal position, supported by webbed straps. A delicate mesh of golden wiring encased each of them, from throat to ankles, in a pulsating electronic womb.

"I *know* those faces!" whispered Francis. "I've seen them before."

"On scanboards at DS." Logan nodded. "Runners who got away."

"So they didn't vanish after all!"

No, thought Logan, they're here—all of them—

taken up to this skycity by Sturdivent's "Gods" to satisfy the Master's sexual desires. *All* of them . . .

Including Jessica!

She lay just below him, her body cocooned in
metal filaments, her eyes closed in dreaming sleep.

A robot guard walked the rows, checking, adjust-
ing body-contact points, making certain that each female was properly tuned to the machine that spun out
endless electronic dreams.

Logan gestured Francis toward the exit.

Back on the walkway, Logan did not mention
having recognized Jessica, but his face was tight-set; he
knew he must find a way to release her. He could not
abandon her here.

"Change of plan," he said. "We don't leave the
city."

Francis stared at him. "But that's the *only* way! If
we don't alert DS to what's happening up here—then
Sturdivent wins! He's ready to make his move."

"There's another way," said Logan. "We'll do it
another way."

The two unit robots assigned to guard the Dreamers were Q-9 W2 models, the latest in the Q-Series
Defense Machine development line. In outer appear-
ance they were identical to earlier models: wide, rein-
forced steelloid bodies with featureless mirror-bright
faces behind which computerized relays directed their
actions. In overall design, however, they were much
more sophisticated.

If what you told a robot didn't compute, Logan
knew, you had to destroy it in order to move forward.
And destroying a Q-9 at this point was out of the question. Logic, computable logic, was the best weapon.

The Q-Series machine at the entrydoor leading to
the Dream Chamber asked Logan and Francis why
they wished to enter.

"The Master has sent us," Logan told the robot.
"We are to take one of the Dreamers back to his quar-
ters under our personal escort."

"I have not been notified in advance," said the robot. "That is customary. I am always notified."

"In this case prior notification is not required," said Logan. "Not when one of the Elite Gods is given a direct order by Sturdivent. We were given that order and we are obeying it. Admit us."

Logic.

The robot admitted them.

Inside, as they moved toward the rows of sleeping women, the inner guard approached them. He had been cleared to deal with them automatically.

"I must warn you," he said, "that when a subject is removed from Dreamstate she must undergo a revival period of one hour in order to restore full physical and mental capability."

"Understood," said Logan.

"Might I then suggest," said the robot, "that you make your selection and return in one hour for her. She will then be totally receptive and functional."

"Sturdivent wants her *now*," said Logan. "The revival period must be bypassed. We are under direct orders to bring her to the Master without delay."

"Very well," said the machine. "But she will not be immediately responsive to sexual stimulation. You are willing to assume total responsibility for this?"

Logan nodded.

"Then please make your selection."

They moved along the rows, past the sleeping women, each young, firm-breasted, beautiful.

"This one," said Logan, touching Jessica's shoulder.

"Number 43." The guard nodded. "I shall disconnect, and bring her to you."

And as the robot began the process of dream-disconnection, Francis questioned Logan: "Why choose Doyle's sister? I thought you told me you weren't involved with her."

"Why *not* choose Doyle's sister?" Logan answered in a hard tone. "It makes no difference which woman we take. The idea is to reach Sturdivent."

"*Your* idea," Francis reminded him. "I liked mine better."

Logan realized he was pushing Francis. Ease

off, he told himself; you can't afford to alienate him.
This won't work without him. You can't do it alone.

Logan modified his tone, still speaking quietly but
with the edge removed. "This will work. I know it will.
Trust me, Francis."

"We'll see."

And he measured Logan with a long, hard glance.

Jessica was theirs now. Dressed erotically in a
scented loverobe, wearing soft slippers, her hair loose
and free-falling, she walked with Logan and Francis in
hazed half-sleep, her mind still fogged, eyes unfocused.
She did not speak as they guided her into the waiting
sky vehicle.

Logan wanted to hold her, comfort her, to eliminate the mental barrier between them—but could do
none of these things. To Francis, she was an escaped
runner, marked for death after her use as a key to
Sturdivent. I'll have to kill him to save Jess, Logan
knew. But not yet.

Francis had been most resourceful in stealing the
skycraft. By morning, when it would be missed, this
would all be over, one way or another.

Logan appreciated the irony in their situation:
Sturdivent is using us, or *thinks* he is; I'm using Francis and Francis is using Jessica. And, behind it all, the
aliens are using me. . . .

Madness. A game of life and death, played across
two worlds, with the final resolution at hand.

THE WOUNDED BEAST

Inside, as the skycraft moved swiftly through the night city on the way to Sturdivent, Francis brought out two burnguns, handing one to Logan.

"Where did you get these?"

"Weapons storage," replied Francis. "Same place I got the skybug. You said we'd need weapons."

"I told you we'd take them from Sturdivent once we're there."

"Too risky. We might have to shoot our way in. I figure he'll be a tough man to reach."

"You're wrong," said Logan. "Here, in his little kingdom, he has absolutely nothing to fear. Who's going to harm the Master? Every human in Nirvana is brainwashed, and no robot is going to attack him. And that's what will make my plan work. He's prepared, defensively, for a possible outside assault—but we hit from *inside*."

"We just walk right in."

"Exactly." Logan put aside the burngun. "Jessica will get us to Sturdivent. And when we go in, we go in clean. No guns."

With a shrug, Francis took the burner from his belt and laid it beside Logan's weapon.

On the roof, as they left the skycraft, Sturdivent's chief house robot formally questioned their arrival. The robot was most polite to these Elite Gods, but he was confused. It was not uncommon that a Dreamer be brought to the Master for late-night pleasure, but the female was always accompanied by other robots. Gods did not accompany Dreamers. As the robot carefully explained, this was not customary.

"The Master personally directed us to bring this Dreamer to him," Logan said in a flat tone, keeping all emotion out of his voice. It was essential that the robot continue to believe them under basic mind-control.

"Not customary," repeated the house machine.

"It is his will and our duty," Francis added. "It would be most unwise if you did not take us to the Master. He would be greatly displeased."

The robot reacted to these key words, and the questioning ended. They were led into the main building, through a labyrinth of corridors, to the personal night chambers of Sturdivent.

Jessica moved with them, docile, easily controlled. Logan looked into her eyes, sought for a flicker of recognition there, but her expression remained vacant, tranquil, childlike. Her body was here, but her mind was with the machine.

I'll get you through this, Jess, Logan silently promised her; I'll get you back to Earth safely, and I'll smash the system that tried to kill you! The aliens picked me for this job, and I'll *do* it!

The house robot reached toward a metal stud set into a tall bronzed door. "I shall inform the Master that you have arrived."

"That will not be necessary," said Logan. "He is expecting us. Just open the door."

"The Master's door is never locked, but no one may enter unannounced. It is the rule, and the rule cannot be—"

The metallic voice ceased abruptly as Francis fired a prime heatcharge into the robot's back.

"I figured you might be wrong about the guns." Francis grinned. "I brought mine along."

Logan eased open the bronze door. "We could have made it inside without killing the robot," he said tightly. "Now we've lost our advantage."

Francis pushed Jess in ahead of him. "We can use her as a shield, let her take the first shot. Save us killing her later."

Logan glared at him, said nothing. He wouldn't let that happen, even if he had to—

Suddenly they were facing the Master.

Sturdivent stood in a thickly draped archway, in a jeweled nightrobe, a heatgun in his right hand.

Logan stepped toward him, smiling.

"What's hapening here?" Sturdivent asked.

"We did not mean to startle you, Master," said Logan. "But we have brought one of the Dreamers for your pleasure. We mean no disrespect by our intrusion." Logan kept his face expressionless, spacing his words in a flat, mind-drugged monotone.

Behind Jessica, masked by her body, Logan saw Francis slip the burnweapon under his tunic. Had Sturdivent seen the gun?

No—he was totally intent on Jessica, devouring her beauty with his dark eyes. Now he swung his gaze to Logan. "A noise . . . I heard a loud noise from the corridor."

"The woman is still in partial Dreamstate," said Logan. "She stumbled and fell."

"We trust we have not disturbed you, Master," said Francis abjectly. "It is our intent only to further your pleasure."

And Logan followed up smoothly: "The only way we knew to express our gratitude for your generosity toward us. As Elite Gods, we used our authority with the robots to bring you this special gift. Were we wrong in doing so, Master? Are you angry with us?"

Their act was working. Sturdivent relaxed, slipping the gun into a pocket of his robe. His eyes were again on Jessica. "This female . . . is extraordinary," he declared softly. "I am pleased that you have brought her."

Sturdivent approached Jess, pulled her body close to his, running his hands over her full breasts beneath the loverobe. He tipped her chin up, kissed her deeply, his tongue probing her open mouth. She submitted numbly, mechanically, eyes clouded as Sturdivent began peeling the robe from her shoulders.

"You may go now," he said, without taking his eyes from Jessica.

Behind him, at a signal, Francis passed his burngun to Logan.

Aware of their silence, Sturdivent turned to them, anger flaring in his voice: "You heard me! Do as I say!"

In one short, lunging step, Logan reached Sturdivent, jabbing the heatgun hard into the flesh of his throat. "No! You do as *we* say, you slimy sonofabitch!"

Francis plunged his right hand into Sturdivent's robe, pulling the beamweapon from his pocket.

Jessica watched all this with empty, dreaming eyes.

"All right now, *Master* . . ." and Logan used the word with bitter contempt, "you take us exactly where we tell you."

"And you take us *now*," added Francis.

Sturdivent was flushed with shock and anger; his face muscles worked spasmodically as his pale hands clenched and unclenched. He knew he could do nothing. They'd burn him down if he resisted. The hate in Logan's eyes told him that.

Francis turned on Jessica, leveling the burngun at her. "Time to die, runner!" He grinned at Logan. "And *this* time she won't vanish!"

"Wait." ordered Logan, stepping between them. "I want her alive . . . for now."

"But why?"

"To testify at DS. Against Sturdivent."

"*We* can do that. She's no good to us now."

"She's my responsibility," said Logan, keeping Sturdivent within gunrange as he spoke. "I say she goes with us."

Francis scowled. "I don't like it."

"There's no time to argue this," snapped Logan. "We know what we have to do. Let's do it."

Francis sighed, moved to Sturdivent, nudged him with the gun. "All right, let's move."

With a beamgun tight against his ribs, Sturdivent took them down a snaking series of corridors and work tunnels to their predetermined destination: the Central Power Control Unit.

All guards and technicians were dismissed without explanation. No one in Nirvana dared question the Master's direct order.

Logan slidelocked the chamber door, turning to face Sturdivent. The area crackled with harnessed energy; its main control board flickered and sizzled with electronic life. Logan could sense the heartbeat of the vast city within this humming room.

"You know what we want," he said.

"But I'm not a control tech," objected Sturdivent. "I can't do it."

"He's lying," said Francis. "He helped design this unit."

Logan placed the barrel of his weapon against Sturdivent's forehead. His tone was ice: "If you don't do as we say, you *know* I'll kill you."

Sturdivent's face was fear-beaded; his lower lip trembled. In resignation, he took over the primary control seat and began togging switches.

"Tell us exactly what you're doing," said Logan.

"I'm doing what you asked—bringing it to manual," explained Sturdivent. "Then I'll reverse the gravity drive and take the city down under personal control. It's not programmed for automatic descent."

"All right," said Logan.

"This is precise work . . . I'll need some help."

Francis took over the second control chair. "Tell me what to do," he said.

Sturdivent gave him detailed instructions, while Logan hovered at his shoulder, eyes intent on the descent dial. The city was now lowering toward Earth, dropping down through its artificial cloud cover, descending steadily toward the Valley of Kings.

Behind them, unobserved, Jessica was slowly backing toward the door. She had reached a mental anxiety state; her machine-dazed mind was telling her that something was wrong. I must help the Master! These men are trying to harm him. They must be stopped.

She edged back another foot, reached the door, released the slidelock—just as Logan pivoted toward her, shouting words she didn't understand. Jessica slipped through the door, crying out for the robot guards.

"Damn you, Logan! I warned you about her!" shouted Francis, twisting to fire at an advancing robot. The machine exploded under the heatcharge—as two more guards rushed forward.

Logan triggered the burner, bringing both of them down in ruin, but another robot was firing from the open doorway—and a laser charge sliced past Logan's head into the main control bank, setting off warning lights and alarms.

Francis managed to slidelock the door again, and now rushed to Sturdivent, who was fighting to maintain a stable altitude.

"How bad?" asked Francis.

"I think I can hold it," said Sturdivent. "The gravity unit is still intact."

For Logan, it was over. He'd lost. No way to escape now, even if they got down safely. Whole city on alert. No way out. No way to save Jess. Robots at the door with beamers, cutting their way inside. Time running out.

Can't get back home. My Earth lost to me forever. Jaq lost. Never see Jess again. Mission a failure. Death waiting.

He could do one thing. He could see to it that this foul kingdom died with him; he could destroy the evil it represented, the perversion and power. . . .

This one final thing he could do.

"Collision course!" he shouted, gun on Sturdivent. "Set it!"

"What?" Sturdivent swung away from the controls. "You can't—"

"I said *kill* it!" ordered Logan. "Crash the city!"

Francis looked stunned. "Logan, what are you—"

Logan didn't wait. He threw his body across the power deck, jamming the grav-control bar full-forward.

The room tipped crazily. Sirens and alarms shrieked at them. The three men were spill-tumbled into the forward end of the room like broken dolls. . . .

An immense, wounded sky beast, the city angled

sharply earthward. Shearing off the great head of the Sphinx as it scythed down, it slammed into the desert floor in a gigantic eruption of exploding buildings, flying metal, and sharded glass; towers collapsed; streets heaved upward, splitting and rupturing; mile-high sunshields folded into themselves, cracking and shuddering ... as the giant skycity convulsed and died.

SURPRISE AND TREACHERY

Dawn.

A slow-rising wind. The Egyptian sun, tilting above the horizon in the Valley of Kings, striking fire reflections from the shattered sky ruin spread across the face of the desert.

No sound. No movement.

Sturdivent: dead, crushed by the city he ruled.

Logan: badly wounded, weakened by blood loss.

Jessica: unconscious, half-buried, lying on her back in the mounded sand next to a broken-bodied robot guard.

Logan staggered to her, cradling her head, smoothing sand from her cheek. Her eyes opened, and she knew him, sobbed his name, reached out to touch, gently, his blood-mapped face. . . . The effects of the machine were gone; she was mentally strong once again.

"Logan!"

The word was a shout, a hard, angry sound. A voice Logan instantly recognized.

Francis.

He moved away from Jess to face this gaunt-bodied killer, this man who would surely now, take his life, burn it away in the heatcharge from the leveled gun.

"It's ended, Francis . . . Sturdivent's dead. And the computers died with the city. DS can't exist without them. The system will disintegrate. It will die as the city died. It's all over."

Francis smiled. His clothing was torn; his skin was bruised; a slight cut bled along his left leg, but he was basically unmarked by the crash.

He was calm, certain of his moves, as Logan swayed in the rising heat, his blood pulsing black and steady into the sand.

"I don't care about the death of this system," Francis said. "No, Logan—it's *your* death I care about. They sent me to kill you and now I will."

"I don't—" Logan blinked at him. *"Who* sent you?"

"Them," said Francis softly. "The same ones— from the ship. I've been one step ahead of you all the way." He smiled. "How do you think I knew so much about the city . . . the Dreamers . . . the Central Power Unit . . . ? *They* told me; they knew all about Sturdivent, from beginning."

"And . . . the drug . . . how you resisted it . . ."

"With *their* shielding—just as you did."

Logan stared at him. "Are you . . . from this planet?"

"No. Another Earth. A third parallel world. The aliens took me, gave me a mission, set me against you. Once you're dead, they'll take me back. They promised that. They'll come for me. At your death, I'm free!"

He raised the beamgun.

And died.

Burned where he stood by the robot guard's weapon in Jessica's hand.

Logan turned to her, trying to speak. His throat muscles moved convulsively. A blood film of weakness hazed his eyes. He stumbled toward Jess, a leg collapsing beneath him. He sprawled into the sand.

She reached out to touch him. "You've won, Logan. The aliens will come for *you* now. You did what they asked you to do."

He shook his head weakly. "Can't . . . can't leave . . . without you . . . love . . . you."

"I know," she said softly, holding him. "I know you love me—as I love you—but you also love the *other* me as much or more. And she will bear your child. . . . You must go back to her."

"Can't . . . leave you . . . to die."

"I won't die now. What you said about the system is true. It's finished . . . I'll survive." She kissed him, touching his fevered lips with hers. "But I'll never forget you. I'll always love you . . . always!"

"Jess . . . Jess . . ."

They embraced—but even as she held him he was changing, dissolving in her arms, losing his physical form. . . .

They were taking him.

Jessica stepped back, tears in her eyes, speaking his name.

He was gone.

Only the blooded sand remained to mark his passage.

He became aware of light: concentrated, all-encompassing, as if the inside of his skull generated its own painfully sharp illumination.

Logan opened his eyes, blinked rapidly, squinting against the radiance.

The resilient surface under his body: medtable.

The subtly curving silver walls rising around him: starship.

The source of light, sunlike and intense: aliens.

We have brought you back, Logan. We have honored our agreement.

Logan sat up, slid from the table to stand facing them. Behind the shielding crystal, the three alien light-forms flickered and coalesced.

His wounds were healed, the clothes he wore, his own. He drew slow fingers across his face.

Restored, they told him. *You are exactly as you were when you left your Earth.*

"And . . . the other Logan?"

Thanks to you, he has been returned to his home planet. He retains life through your success.

"What about Jessica: I didn't want to leave her there . . . will she survive?"

We cannot read futures. But she lives now. And she is strong, resourceful. You need not concern yourself about her.

Anger began building within Logan; his sense of personal betrayal asserted itself. He had been lied to, cruelly tricked.

"You knew about Godbirth from the start—about Sturdivent, the city, all of it!"

Yes. We had that knowledge.

"And about the female runners—where they were taken and what was done to them . . ."

We knew.

Logan's face tightened. His voice was bitter with accusation: "You sent Francis to kill me!"

Of course. We do not deny this.

"Why did he wait? He could have killed me long before he tried."

That was part of our agreement with him. He was forbidden to kill you until the Godbirth process was completed, and until you were free of the city.

"That explains why he was so anxious to guide me through the ritual and then have me leave with him."

Precisely. In killing you, Francis would have achieved his mission. He would then have been safely returned to his world.

"You were monitoring three Earths, not two, and he came from this third Earth?"

Yes.

"And the *other* Francis?"

Dead, naturally. We destroyed him—just as we would have destroyed your duplicate had you failed.

Logan paced the chamber, trying to control his rising anger. He turned back toward the tri-blazed light: "And Phedra?"

We arranged for her to betray you in Arcade.

"Kirov . . . Monte Carlo?"

We planted the desire for a Sandman's Gun in

Kirov's mind. In order to make things a bit more difficult for you.

"When you warned me to stay away from Jessica —you actually *wanted* me to see her, fall in love with her!"

True. The interaction between you generated pleasure for us.

Logan was trying to understand it all. Now he hesitated, confused. "But you weren't there. How could anything I did on Earth afford you pleasure here?"

We were there, Logan. When we altered your body we implanted certain highly sensitive monitoring devices beneath your skin surface. Thus, we were able to see through your body, to experience fear, anger, passion—just as you experienced them.

A pause. Then: *We particularly enjoyed your encounter with the barracuda. Really quite stimulating.*

Logan fought back the revulsion welling up in his mind. He felt totally betrayed; he had been grossly manipulated.

"My mission—whether or not I destroyed Sturdivent's grip on Earth—that never really mattered to you, did it?"

How one small planet is controlled, and by whom, is of no concern to us. In presenting your mission, we simply utilized your limited sense of human morality.

"If all this is so unimportant to you, why did you bother to bring me back!"

We had agreed to do so. And we keep our agreements.

The light-forms were fading; the crystal lost its radiance, began to break apart. Logan ran forward to the dissolving crystal, suddenly desperate. "You can't go now! You can't leave me here—in this ship!"

To have done all this, to have fought his way clear of Earth, and to end up here, on this starcraft, drifting the stars forever, was too horrible to contemplate! Surely, they were not this cruel, this indifferent to all that he had done. . . .

The crystal was gone.

The aliens were gone.

Logan was alone.

Then, to calm him, to ease his darkest fears, their voice flowed into his mind: *We keep our agreements.*

And he, too, began to change . . . to dissolve. . . .

Home!

His world . . . his Earth!

On the lawn of his house near Maincamp. Sitting at the controls of the silent paravane, the food crates beside him, with all of it done—the horror of the Jamaican deeps . . . the fall from the cliffs at Monte Carlo . . . the entrapment inside the cave at Kilimanjaro . . . the drugged nightmares . . . the death of the skycity . . . the terrors and the hunts and the killing . . . the struggle to survive—all of it, over and done, with him here, safe, back home at last with . . .

Jess!

She was walking toward him from the house.

Walking? Why isn't she running? Why is she so calm, so unemotional?

He was back from the dead, wasn't he? . . . home again after an impossible journey across space and time!

He jumped down from the control pod, taking her into his arms, heart racing, eyes blurred with tears. He couldn't speak; the words of joy were locked in his throat.

She looked at him oddly, head canted. "Why are you back so soon?"

"Soon? But I was—"

"You just took off—and now you're back," she said. "I didn't even hear you land."

He stared at her, suddenly aware of the final irony—that time, as it is measured in one universe, does not exist in the next; that here, on this Earth, his whole incredible adventure had taken place in *nontime!*

"Why *did* you come back?" Jess asked, with a puzzled frown.

"For you." He smiled. "For you, and Jaq. I want you *with* me. Will you come with me?"

She smiled back at him. "All right . . . I'll make the flight to Chicago. I'll go with you." She looked down, placed a hand at her rising stomach. *"We'll* go with you." There was puzzlement in her eyes. "But are you *sure* there's nothing wrong?"

"No," he said, smiling foolishly. "Nothing's wrong. Not now!"

And Logan held her . . . them . . . Jessica and Jaq . . . close against his fast-beating heart.

ABOUT THE AUTHOR

WILLIAM F. NOLAN is the author of over thirty books, half of which are in the science fiction genre. He also writes mysteries, and was twice awarded the Edgar Allan Poe Special Award from the Mystery Writers of America. His work has appeared in over a hundred publications, ranging from *The Magazine of Fantasy and Science Fiction* to *Playboy*, and he has also been a book and magazine editor. Mr. Nolan has written several television movies, including *The Norliss Tapes*, *Trilogy of Terror* and *Melvin Purvis, G-Man*, and his screenplays include *Burnt Offerings* and *The Legend of Machine-Gun Kelly*. One of his television films won the Golden Medallion, presented at the Fourth International Festival of Science Fiction and Fantasy Films in Paris. His work has been widely translated and selected for numerous "best" anthologies. In addition, Mr. Nolan has been awarded an honorary doctorate for his lifelong contributions to the field of science fiction by the American River College in Sacramento, California. He lives with his wife, Kam, in Woodland Hills, California.

OUT OF THIS WORLD!

That's the only way to describe Bantam's great series of science fiction classics. These space-age thrillers are filled with terror, fancy and adventure and written by America's most renowned writers of science fiction. Welcome to outer space and have a good trip!

]	13179	**THE MARTIAN CHRONICLES** by Ray Bradbury	$2.25
]	13695	**SOMETHING WICKED THIS WAY COMES** by Ray Bradbury	$2.25
]	14323	**STAR TREK: THE NEW VOYAGES** by Culbreath & Marshak	$2.25
]	13260	**ALAS BABYLON** by Pat Frank	$2.25
]	14124	**A CANTICLE FOR LEIBOWITZ** by Walter Miller, Jr.	$2.50
]	11175	**THE FEMALE MAN** by Joanna Russ	$1.75
]	13312	**SUNDIVER** by David Brin	$1.95
]	12957	**CITY WARS** by Dennis Palumbo	$1.95
]	11662	**SONG OF THE PEARL** by Ruth Nichols	$1.75
]	13766	**THE FARTHEST SHORE** by Ursula LeGuin	$2.25
]	13594	**THE TOMBS OF ATUAN** by Ursula LeGuin	$2.25
]	13767	**A WIZARD OF EARTHSEA** by Ursula LeGuin	$2.25
]	13563	**20,000 LEAGUES UNDER THE SEA** by Jules Verne	$1.75
]	12655	**FANTASTIC VOYAGE** by Isaac Asimov	$1.95

Buy them at your local bookstore or use this handy coupon for ordering:

FANTASY AND SCIENCE FICTION FAVORITES

Bantam brings you the recognized classics as well as the current favorites in fantasy and science fiction. Here you will find the beloved Conan books along with recent titles by the most respected authors in the genre.

☐	01166	URSHURAK	
		Bros. Hildebrandt & Nichols	$8.95
☐	13610	NOVA Samuel R. Delany	$2.25
☐	13534	TRITON Samuel R. Delany	$2.50
☐	13612	DHALGREN Samuel R. Delany	$2.95
☐	12018	CONAN THE SWORDSMAN #1	
		DeCamp & Carter	$1.95
☐	12706	CONAN THE LIBERATOR #2	
		DeCamp & Carter	$1.95
☐	12970	THE SWORD OF SKELOS #3	
		Andrew Offutt	$1.95
☐	14321	THE ROAD OF KINGS #4	
		Karl E. Wagner	$2.25
☐	14127	DRAGONSINGER Anne McCaffrey	$2.50
☐	14204	DRAGONSONG Anne McCaffrey	$2.50
☐	12019	KULL Robert E. Howard	$1.95
☐	10779	MAN PLUS Frederik Pohl	$1.95
☐	11736	FATA MORGANA William Kotzwinkle	$2.95
☐	11042	BEFORE THE UNIVERSE	$1.95
		Pohl & Kornbluth	
☐	13680	TIME STORM Gordon R. Dickson	$2.50
☐	13400	SPACE ON MY HANDS Frederic Brown	$1.95